DADDY'S DESTRUCTION

UNIQUE ARTISTIC

While some incidents in this book are true, the names and personal characteristics of those described have been changed in order to protect their privacy. Any resemblance to persons living or dead is entirely incidental and unintentional.

PRINTED IN THE UNITED STATES OF AMERICA

ISBN- 9798746572967

Cover Designer: Creative -Art086

Author: LaCoya Foxx

Publisher: BN Publications

CHAPTER ONE

I rolled over in my California king bed to an empty spot, where the hell is my husband, I thought. I stretched and went to brush my teeth and wash my face. As I stared at my reflection, I couldn't help but to reflect on my life.

My name is Yatise, but everyone calls me Yotti. I'm 24 years old and in law school, married with three kids. I live in a four bedroom 2 1/2 bath house. Just like everyone else I went through hell and hot water to get where I am, and I don't regret any of it I'm finally happy. Let me tell y'all about myself and where I came from.

Money: (Yotti's daddy)

I stood up and stretched with my 6"1 frame, I looked over at my man's Ceaser who was rolling a blunt. Let's roll my nigga we gotta make dis drop, I told him.

He stuck the blunt behind his ear and stood up. We hopped in his Yukon fired up the blunt and pulled off. We made small talk about our plans when my phone started ringing.

Yo, I answered without looking at it.

Your daughter is on her way, a woman said before hanging up.

Fuck, I mumbled.

Turn around yo, baby girl on the way, I said to Ceaser, as he busted a U heading towards the hospital.

He dropped me off and went to handle our business. I made my way through the hospital till reaching the receptionist desk.

Hey how you are doing, I'm looking for Nyla James. I said to the receptionist.

She looked up at me with an attitude, but when she saw me, her demeanor changed. My tall frame, funny colored eyes, and curly hair attracted a lot of females.

I'm fine, what did u say her name was again, she said.

Nyla James, I said as she begins typing on the computer.

What's your relationship to the patient? she asked looking at me with a smile.

I'm the child's father, I responded.

She's in room 7323, down the hall to the left, she said as she pointed.

Thanks ma, I said.

No problem sir.

Your gorgeous ma, for real, I told her as she blushed, and I walked off.

When I got to the room Nayla's momma was outside talking on the phone.

How you are doing Mrs. James, I asked her.

She just looked at me and rolled her eyes, that lady can't stand me for denying Nyla's baby, but how can she blame me, Nyla disappeared, and called me six months later talm bout she pregnant and it's a girl.

I walked in the room and from the looks of things I could tell she had already had the baby.

Bout time big head, my older sister Chell said as she stood up to hug me.

Wats going on sis, I asked her as I kissed her forehead.

I looked at Nyla who looked as if she's just had a rough day in court.

Wats up girl, I said walking towards her laughing to give her a hug.

I'm tired, and hungry, she whined.

I just ordered her room service, my sister Chell spoke up.

Where is the baby? I asked I was past ready to see her, I wanted to know if she was mine.

She's in the nursery, I will take you, my sister said as she stood up and handed me the daddy band.

When I saw her, I knew indeed she was mine, from her thick curly hair, to those small pink lips, she had her mama nose tho, but when she opened her eyes, I couldn't deny her if I wanted to with those big funny colored eyes. The minute I got her in the room I scooped her out the bassinet and plated kisses all over her face. On August 4, 1991 the love of my life was born.

I love her already, my Yotti, I said rocking her back and forth while looking into her eyes

CHAPTER TWO

Daddy, my baby screamed as I walked through the door. I scooped her up and planted kisses all over her face, I missed you daddy stink, look what daddy got you while I was in Detroit. I said as I put her down so she could play with her gifts.

I done told you about all this stuff you keep getting her money, my baby mama Nyla said.

I'm just making sure my baby know daddy got her, I told her as I helped Yotti with her gifts.

No, you're just spoiling her, she stated with an attitude.

It's been two years, and I haven't missed a beat in my daughter's life, every time I get something for my stink her momma always got something to say, if I didn't know no better, I would think she was jealous of my baby.

I walked towards Nyla and gently grabbed her pudgy nose, let me find out you jealous of my baby, I said with a smirk, but I was serious as hell.

She rolled her eyes and walked to the back, I looked down at Yotti who was occupied with her gifts and followed Nyla to the back. I walked in her room and she was standing in the mirror pulling her hair up. I had a wife but for some reason I couldn't leave baby moms alone, Nyla was short, brown skin, with full lips and a pudgy nose. Although she wasn't as cute, she was thick as fuck and could make that ass clap like no other. I walked behind her wrapping my arms around her waist.

You want some of daddy attention to, I said while pulling her satin robe open, I ran my tongue from her shoulder blade to her ear lobe, she arched her back, I smirked cuz I knew that was her spot. She turned around to face me, I licked my lips as I looked at her with a matching bra and panties set on. She reached down and unbuckled my pants she got down on her knees pulling my pants down, taking all of me in her mouth. I bit down on my bottom lip, as my man begin to throb against her moist lips she moaned as she flicked her tongue across my head, as prenup oozed out.

Damn girl, I moaned as I gripped her head gliding my stick in and out her mouth.

She stood up, and I picked her up sitting her on the dresser, I slid her panties off and ran my finger across her wet kat, I Put a rubber on, pulled her to the edge of the dresser while going inside her with deep long strokes. She thru her head back as she begins to moan, while gripping the edge of the dresser so hard her fingers were turning white.

Yes! Daddy right there, she moaned while opening her legs wider so I can go deeper.

I felt my dick throb as she tightened her walls around it.

Mommy, we heard Yotti say as she busted the room door open, I quickly pulled out, and pulled my pants up, Nyla climbed off the dresser, while closing her robe.

What's wrong baby, she asked her.

Body at the door, she said while smiling, and looking back and forth between us.

Nyla tied her robe tight while going to answer the door.

Go wit mommy stink, I told her as I headed towards the bathroom in Nyla's room.

She ran out the room as fast as her Lil legs will take her, I went in the bathroom pulled my condom off, and washed my nuts, before heading out the room.

What the fuck you mean you ain't got time to talk to me right now, I heard some tall man yell in Nyla face, as she blocked him from getting in the door.

What fuckin part don't you understand nigga I'm busy, she yelled just as loud as he yelled at her.

Yotti was standing behind Nyla's leg I tapped her and pointed towards her room, and she took off running closing the door behind her.

Fuck you bitch, he said.

I slightly moved Nyla over, and pulled him in by his shirt, making him fall to the ground I had him pinned down by his shirt, Nyla walked around us shutting, and locking the door.

What the fuck you just called my baby mama, I said thru clinched teeth, while sticking my strap in his face.

I'm sorry dog, I didn't know, he said as I felt his body shaking under me.

I smacked him twice in the face with my gun, drawing blood from his mouth, and nose, open the door, I growled at Nyla, she did as I lifted him up by his shirt, pushing him out the door, he stumbled on the way out, I kicked him dead in his ass causing him to fall, don't bring yo broke ass here nomo punk ass nigga, I said as he stumbled down the steps to his car.

I shut the door and locked it heading towards the bathroom, without saying anything to Nyla.

Sorry about that, Nyla said while walking in the bathroom wrapping her arms around me as I wiped blood off my gun.

Whatever, I said while putting my gun in my waist, I brushed passed her headed to check on my stink.

I walked in Yotti's room, but I didn't see her.

Stink, I called out.

Peek a boo, she said poking her head from under the bed laughing.

I laughed as I pulled her out, give daddy a kiss I gotta go, I told her.

She hugged me tight, and kissed all over my face, I lobe u daddy, she said while laughing.

Love u too be good for yo mama, I told her, and left her room.

Nyla met me at the front door, so were not gonna finish what we started, she asked.

Naw, I got shit to do, don't let me catch that nigga around y'all nomo, I said and walked out without waiting for a response.

CHAPTER THREE

It's been a month since the last time I've been with Money sexually and it's driving me crazy. Somehow his wife found out we were still sleeping together, and now he want even look my way in a sexual manner. I've done everything I could to seduce him, but he pays me no attention, it's always about his "stink". Don't get me wrong I love my daughter, but I can't help but to feel like she's in the way when it comes to me and her father. Better yet it's that bitch Melanie in the way, I don't even know where the hoe came from. I was here before all these bitches, and was there when he didn't have shit, and he repay me by marrying the next trick, and sticking me with a baby. I Dialed his number again for the sixth time hoping he would pick up.

Yo, he answered on the third ring.

Hey, wat you are doing, I asked him.

Working what's going on... Where my stink at, he asked.

I sighed, she's taking a nap, she was asking for you earlier, you should come see her, I told him really wanting him to come see me.

He paused for a minute, aight I'll be there in bout a hour or two, he said.

We said our goodbyes and hung up. I climbed off the couch to go check on the meatloaf in the oven, Yotti wasn't even here, she went with my momma for the weekend, but I've been wanting to feel Money's touch for so long that I was going to do any and everything to get him here. I know he loved my cooking, and meatloaf was his favorite, so I whipped him up a quick meal, and picked out a lingerie so sexy he want resist. An hour and a half later dinner was cooked, I've showered, cleaned, and had our plates made for us. I was in the bathroom freshen up when I heard a knock at the door, I double checked myself in the mirror before opening the door. There he stood with Ceaser right behind him, I rolled my eyes, while tightening my robe up, why this nigga couldn't come by his self.

What's up girl, what are you cooking? he asked walking in looking high as hell.

Meatloaf your plates in the microwave, I said while closing the door behind them.

I walked in the kitchen as money was heating his plate up.

Do you want apples Ceaser? I asked as I begin to fix him a plate.

And you know it, he said while rubbing his hands together.

Where my stink at, money asked while taking a bite from his food.

Ugh momma came and got her bout 30 mins ago, but they should be back soon, I lied

He nodded his head and continued to eat his food. Afterwards they played the Xbox till Ceaser got his baby mama to come get him.

What time u say stink coming, money asked while taking a pull from one of his many blunts.

Um I don't know let me call them, I said while going to the back.

I came back to the living room and made up a story about Yotti helping her bake a cake and its almost ready.

I'm finna take a nap, he said while standing up stretching, and headed towards my room.

Yesss!!!

CHAPTER FOUR

I was in a good sleep when I felt something wet gliding up and down my shift, and a small soft hand massaging my balls, I laid there because it felt good. Then I felt a warm mouth, and tight jaws going to work on my mans, I grabbed the back of her head, as I tried to keep my moans in but it was no use.

Shit.... Fuck girl, damn that feel good, I got out as I felt my nut finna cum.

It shot out and eased down her throat. I opened my eyes, as she stood up, I bit my bottom lip cuz baby moms ain't lost it, she is looking good as fuck right now, it was hard for me not to touch.

C'mer girl, I said as I pulled her on my lap.

She straddled my lap, as she slowly begins to grind on me thru her panties, I pulled her bra off as I ran my tongue around her right nipple, as I massaged the left. After teasing each nipple, causing them to get hard, I ran my hands over her ass, sliding her panties off. She lifted her hips, and was about to slide on, when my phone rung.

Hol up, I said while reaching for my phone.

Can it wait? she asked refusing to move.

Naw watch out, I said while lifting her up by her waist.

Was up baby, I answered the phone for my wife, I looked at Nyla, and she had the biggest mug on her face.

Hey, where are you, she asked.

I came over to see my stink for a minute, I told her.

Um huh, bring yo ass home, before you end up in bed with that slut, she said before hanging up.

I stood up, and pulled my pants up, man where stink at, I asked as I begin putting my shoes on.

Mama called while you were sleep, and said she was gone bring her tomorrow, she said walking towards me.

I laughed as she reached out grabbing my belt buckle.

Naw I gotta go, I said moving her small hand out the way.

Why you gotta do that every time, she asked growing angry.

Do what.... You with the bullshit you knew Yotti wasn't coming back in the first fucking place, I slightly yelled at her.

So, what you tryna say I tricked you to come over here, she asked while shipping her weight from one leg to the other.

That's what the fuck I just said ain't it, I said.

Trick you to come over here for what, I told you mama called me, she said yelling.

I looked at her like she was crazy, who the fuck you think you fooling NY NY, the only phone I heard ringing was mine, ain't nobody called yo dumb ass, I snapped on her I ain't have time to keep playing this Lil game with her.

Her nose begin to flare, I laughed cuz she look sexy ass hell when she mad. I was so caught up in how she looked, that I didn't see her ass swing at me till I felt it in my jaw.

She swung again, but I caught her hand, what the fuck wrong wit chu, I yelled while twisting both her wrist.

You're what's wrong with me, she yelled as tears begin to roll down her face, I don't understand why you keep putting her before me, she said calmer.

She my wife Nyla, I said.

So, the fuck what! I birthed your child, she yelled.

What you want from me Nyla huh, everything you and my daughter need I make sure y'all got that I will never let a muthafuka walking this earth disrespect y'all, you got me in yo corner, I got yo back so why you tripping so hard, I asked her.

Because she's in my place, I'm supposed to be your wife, I was there for you when you didn't have shit! She yelled.

I just looked at her, before turning to head out the room, I opened the front door about to walk out when she grabbed my arm.

Why won't you give me a chance to show you I can be a good wife and mother to yall, she asked as tears streaked her face.

Cuz, I love my wife, and only my wife, from now on when I wanna see Yotti, ima take her with me, I said before leaving.

I made all my pick-ups, and drop offs before heading home, I was sitting in the driveway smoking a blunt on the phone with Ceaser.

Ion no what's going on but these last couple of things been short, he said referring to the dope.

I scratched my chin, tryna figure shit out, aight let me go holla at wifey, and I'll be thru there late night, he knew that meant weneva wifey went to bed.

Aight duce, he said before hanging up.

I hung up, and looked at Mell watch me through the door, I climbed out, and headed in the house. She stood there wearing a pair of mixed match socks, and an oversized t shirt. Unlike Nyla Mell was beautiful, she had caramel colored skin, perfect white teeth, she was slim with long legs and big breast. she rocked a short cut, and always kept it laid. She was smart and loyal, and I loved her.

Was up baby, I said while wrapping my arms around her waist, and bending down to kiss her lips, but she turned her head.

You smell like a bitch, she said before walking of going in the kitchen.

I started to follow her, but I didn't feel like hearing her mouth, telling me to take a shower, so I just went ahead and got in.

CHAPTER FIVE

Yotti:

I laid across my bed patiently waiting on daddy to come get me. It's the beginning of summer break, and I refuse to spend another minute in here with her. I got up to look out my window when I heard a car pull up, it was just troy, one of my mama's guy friends.

Yatise come down here and speak to troy, my momma yelled from downstairs.

I rolled my eyes; she gets on my nerves with that shit. Every nigga she messes with she forces me to like them, she's always tryna turn me against my daddy. I couldn't stand troy, he's always looking at me sexually, and always making slick comments about how, my breast is spreading, or my butts gotten fatter. It irked me to my soul, and one day my mama gone have the nerve to tell me to call him daddy, she done lost her mind. I climbed down the stairs and saw troy sitting on the couch. The minute I walked in his eyesight, his eyes immediately wondered all over my body, I felt so naked, and I was fully clothed. I walked right pass him and into the kitchen.

Ma what time you say daddy was coming, I asked her as she took the pot roast out the oven.

Look don't fucking ask me shit about him, don't even mention his name around me, she snapped on me for no reason.

Ma I just--- I couldn't even get the rest out before she backhanded me right in my mouth.

Close your fuckin mouth, now go clean your face, and come watch this food while I run to the store, she said before leaving, without saying a word, and without taking her perverted ass boyfriend. I wasn't in the bathroom for 30 seconds before troy knocked asking me how long I was gone be there. I waited till I heard him walk down the hallway, I walked out and walked to the kitchen, I pulled out my phone, and called daddy.

Was up stink, he answered on the second ring.

I looked up and saw troy in the doorway staring at me, I felt sick to my stomach.

Hey daddy where are you? I asked while stirring the macaroni.

I'll be there in a few minutes baby, he said.

Daddy can you please hurry, I said as troy walked back to the living room.

I'm on my way baby girl, he said before hanging up.

I kept my phone up to my ear, so troy would think I was still on the phone. I don't know what it is between my mama and daddy, but my mama can't stand him, it doesn't make since to me I'm 14 years old, and you would think they would have learned how to co parent by now. I was so caught up in my own thoughts, that I didn't hear troy come in the kitchen. His big ruff hands grabbed a chunk of my ass, causing me to jump and drop my phone.

Get the fuck off me troy, I yelled while pushing him.

He grabbed my hands, pushing me against the wall. He pressed his body against mine, breathing hot beer in my face.

You can't speak when you see daddy Lil girl, he said while trying to pin my hands above my head.

Just as I was about to say something somebody knocked on the door.

I always speak when I see daddy, I said as a smile grew across my face, I kneed him in the balls, and jogged to the front door. Just as I was reaching to unlock the door, I felt a tug on my hair.

If you tell yo daddy anything, I'ma slit yo mama throat from ear to ear, he said before letting me go and going to sit on the couch like nothing happened.

Hey daddy, I said while wrapping my arms around him tight.

Wasup stink, he said kissing my cheek, and closing the door, where yo mama, he said heading towards the back.

She went to the store, I said before I heard the front door shut. My mother walked in the kitchen, brushed past my daddy to sit the bags down.

Nyla, come here right quick, troy yelled from the living room.

Yatise put that macaroni in the oven to bake, she ordered before leaving the kitchen.

Hurry up and do what yo mama said stink, I'm ready to go I don't like her attitude, my daddy said while shuffling thru the mail on the counter.

I did as he said, then headed up stairs to get my jacket, and purse. I walked back downstairs, and daddy was now standing in the living room talking to mama.

All I'm saying is that you would want to be respected if someone walks in your house, what's wrong with speaking to troy when you come in, my mama said to my daddy.

He looked at her like she done lost her damn mind.

What tha fuck I'ma speak to a nigga that can't even take care of his home for, you sound just as dumb as you look. He semi yelled.

You are speaking on my household like you know something, don't worry about mine they straight, troy said while standing up off the couch.

Fuck you mean they, the only person you need to be concerned about is Nyla, yo mind should be nowea near my daughter, that's my baby I got her, my daddy said, I saw his jaw flinching, so I knew he was mad.

Fuck you nigga, you walk around this mother fucka like somebody pose to be scared of you, ain't nobody scared of yo bit--, was all troy got out before daddy karate chopped him in the throat.

Troy fell holding his throat, tryna catch his breath, daddy looked at me and calmly said, let's go.

I reached for the door, but mama yanked me back by my hair, fuck you think you going, she said while slanging me behind her.

Fuck you got going on Nyla huh, my daddy said stepping towards us.

You don't run shit over here, you don't walk in here disrespecting my man like you king tut or somebody and think you finna take her fast ass out of this house after she been talking back to me, my mama spat standing her ground.

He looked past her, at me and said, what happen to yo lip stink.

Her mouth is what happened, every time she leaves with you and come back, she starts disrespecting me, my mama said while putting her hands on her hips.

Out the corner of my eye I saw troy flash across towards daddy, daddy moved his head just in time to miss Troy's swing. He hit troy in the stomach, causing him to fold, then he swung hard hitting him in the jaw, he hit him so hard you could hear the crack. Troy fell holding his jaw hollering, let's go Yotti, my daddy said calmly. This time my mama didn't put up a fight, she knew when to fuck with my daddy, and when not to.

CHAPTER SIX

Yotti:

The ride to daddy's was silent, except for his phone constantly ringing. We pulled up in the driveway, I saw Melanie's car, and aunt Sonya's. She wasn't really my auntie, her and Mell are really close. I walked in right behind daddy, as Melanie, was walking towards the den. She spent around, and a smile spread across her face.

Hey daddy, she said walking towards my daddy, wrapping her arms around his neck.

He cupped her ass, was up lady, he said before kissing her lips.

Yuck, I said while sticking my finger in my mouth pretending to throw up.

Mell laughed, as she broke their embrace to hug me, she planted kisses all over my face as if I was a baby, I missed you baby.

I know I miss you to ma, I said with a smile. My mama hated the fact that I call Melanie mama to, the first day she heard me say that she beat my ass. But I couldn't help it Mell had just as much impact on my life as my mama, I love Mell just as much as I love my mama, but my mama won't accept that. She tries so hard to turn me against them that its actually pushing me towards them, I mean regardless of how much, I love Mell, or how much Mell does for me, she will never take the place of my mother, but why can't my mother see that.

Mylasia is in your room, go speak to Aunt Sonya first tho, Mell said nodding towards the den.

Please don't forget my event starts in three hours Maurice, I heard Mell tell my daddy as I walked off.

Hey auntie, I said leaning down to kiss her cheek.

Was up boo, she said.

I laughed on my way upstairs, Aunt Sonya was a trip. She was one of those women who acted sophisticated in public but was really ghetto as hell. Her daughter Mylasia, which is my best friend, is the opposite she aint hidden or sugar-coating shit. Mylasia was tall about 5"6 with a mocha-colored skin tone, she was slender with some hips and a nice butt. pigeon toed, with braces, she had long thick hair, but it wasn't a good texture, so she rocked braids majority of the time.

Is that my best bish, mymy said climbing off my bed to hug me.

Hey, my brat, I said as I hugged her.

Knock knock knock

Yes, I responded to the knock at my bedroom door.

The door opened; it was Aunt Sonya.

MyMy I'm leaving, I'll see you Monday, Aunt Sonya said sticking her head in the door.

Bye mama love you, MyMy said to her, aunt Sonya said it back, and left.

Yotti! I could hear my daddy yell from downstairs.

I got up, and went to see what he wanted, I walked thru his big ass house till I finally found him in the bathroom, yes daddy, I said hopping on the bathroom counter.

Fix my tie for me, he said scooting closer to me.

I sighed, what do you want to talk about daddy, I asked as I begin to fix his tie.

How you figure I wanna talk, he asked while holding his neck up.

Because the only time you need help with your tie is when you wanna talk, any other time you get Mell to do it, there I'm finished, I said climbing off the counter.

What you, and yo mama get into it for, he asked while observing his tie in the mirror.

We didn't she just hit me, I said to him.

Don't lie to me stink, she said your mouth has gotten smart has it, he asked

I wouldn't lie to you daddy, I asked what time you were coming to get me, and she just went off, I told him.

Went off like what, what she says, he asked getting angry.

She said quit asking her about you, she don't even want me to mention your name around her, I told him the truth.

Honestly, I was tired of hiding it, I've never once heard Melanie, or my daddy down talk my mother. But she says everything in the world negative about them, and if I even fix my mouth to defend them, she will smack the shit outta me. Don't get me wrong I love her dearly, she is sweet as can be, and always has my back, but it’s like when you mention daddy or Mell, she turns into a different person, and I hated that side of her.

And what you say, he asked while spraying cologne on.

She didn't even let me finish talking, I was gonna say, I just asked what time my daddy was coming, but she smacked me at just, I told him.

He nodded his head, how I look baby girl, he asked me to step back so I could see him.

I smiled, you look good daddy, I told him.

My daddy always looked good, but it was something about him in a suit. I admired him so much I wanted my husband just like him, he's my ideal man, he's a protector, and a provider, and did I mention he puts god first. My daddy does his dirt, and is not perfect, but he knows who to bow down to and that's god.

Thanks stink, I gotta ask you something tho, he said getting more serious.

Was up, I asked hopping back on the counter,

Do you mama leave you at home all the time with her boyfriend, he asked while starring me dead in my face.

No that was her first time, I told him the truth.

Did he do anything to you, say something, look at you funny, touch you anything, he asked me.

Everything in me screamed yes, all the above, but I kept picturing my mama with her head off.

No, I simply said.

He starred me down, I couldn't stand to keep looking at him, and I just lied. I looked away; can I go now.

Yeah, he said before turning to leave. I left out the room only to be stopped by Mell.

Your daddy and I are gonna be out late, so order some pizza, and Kayla's been calling looking for you, where's your phone, she asked while handing me sixty dollars.

Um I broke it earlier, I said

Well, we will get you another one tomorrow, but Kayla said she's coming over, she said while looking over daddy who had just walked up.

You look sexy in a suit daddy, Mell said to my daddy.

Okay I love you guys see y'all later, I said pushing them towards the door.

Hold up, how you break your phone, my daddy asked spinning around to face me.

Maurice let's go before I'm late, Mell spoke up.

He looked at me hard, before leaving, he knows something. Whenever he feels like I'm hiding something, he asks questions, and puts my answers together like a puzzle till he figures out what's going on. Crazy part is he's always right, and it never take him long to figure out.

CHAPTER SEVEN

Money:

It was hard for me to focus on the event I was attending, for my wife. My mind was focused on Yotti. After going around the room speaking to the important people, Mell excused herself to the restroom, I made my way out to the balcony, speaking to people who stopped me along the way. I pulled out my phone and dialed my godson Hustla number. Hustla is Ceaser son, Ceaser got locked up two years ago, doing a eight year bid. I keep hustla up under me, I make sure his family straight.

Wasup Unk, he answered on the third ring.

Was gud, I need you to do something for me, I told him.

I don't know what's going on between Yotti and that fuck boy Troy, but I saw it in her eyes that she was hiding something. Why I don't know, she knows she can tell me anything and I got her back. Maybe he threatened her or something, whatever the case maybe this nigga got to be a fool to think he gone get away with doing anything to my daughter.

What's that Unk, he asked while cutting the music down in the background.

I need you to watch some troy nigga for me and tell your brother to take over what you're doing for me now, ima text you the address, I said before ending the call, I sent the address, just as Mell walked up to me.

There you are, I want you to meet my new associates, she said while pulling me back inside.

Yotti:

I was laying across my bed eating pizza, while MyMy sat at the computer, and my big cousin Kayla sat on the phone with her boyfriend Kai.

Kayla was my daddy's older sister Michelle's only child. Kayla was high yellow, although we both were mixed with Puerto Rician and black my skin tone had more of a tint to it. She was as tall as MyMy, with a small waistline and hips like a belly dancer. She always wore her hair in a big bushy curly fro with a middle part. sounds a mess right, but it was cute especially with her natural hair color being honey blonde. She had big brown eyes, and a beauty mark that sat above her lip.

No, she's 15, Kayla lied about my age to whoever she was talking to, her and her boyfriend was tryna hook me up with his friend.

Don't lie Kayla, I whispered to her. She waived me off as she continued to talk on the phone.

Hold on here she goes, she said handing me the phone.

I rolled my eyes at her before taking the phone, hello, I said putting a Lil sexy behind my voice.

Was up ma, what you got going on, he asked sounding sexy as ever, I hated when people call me ma, but he sounded sexy saying it.

Hey... What you say your name was again, I asked him.

Dee, what's yours, he asked me.

Yotti, I answered

And how old you say you was, he asked.

I'm 14, and you, I asked him back.

I thought you was 15 why yo cousin tell that lie, he asked.

Kayla smacked my arm for telling, I couldn't help but to laugh. I mean I will be 15 soon, how old are you.

16, he responded.

Is that all you act like you're like 18 or something, I said to him and he busted out laughing.

Right, I did say sumtin like you was young ass hell, but I really don't care for this blind date type of shit, so when can I see you, he asked getting straight to the point.

Um I will probably be free tomorrow, I told him.

Cool can I get your number or something, so I can call you, he asked.

Um no but I will get yours from Kayla, I said.

Damn it’s like that, he said while laughing, that's cool I guess, you better call me to girl, he said still laughing.

I will I said before handing Kayla her phone back.

We chilled until we fell asleep. This next morning, I woke up to the smell of bacon. I climbed over MyMy and went into the bathroom to wash my face and brush my teeth. I was expecting to see Mell cooking but instead saw my daddy.

Morning daddy, I said while going in the fridge to get some orange juice.

Morning stink, he said while pouring eggs on a plate.

Are you still gonna take us over aunt Chell's today? I asked him as I begin to fix my plate.

Yo mama called, you gotta go home today, he said while heading out the kitchen.

I sat my half-fixed plate down, and followed him to his room, for what daddy, I always spend summers with you, please don't make me go hone now, I damn near begged.

Why you don't wanna go home, he asked while handing Mell her plate.

I just don't daddy, I wanna stay here with y'all, do I have to have a reason to wanna spend more time with y'all, I asked him.

He bit into his bacon, well you going, only for today, yo mama want you there for yo granny's birthday dinner, he said.

And when you get finished eating go get dress so we can get you a phone, Mell said while eating.

I did as they said eat and got dressed. They dropped mymy, and Kayla of at aunt Chell's. We got my phone and headed to my mamas.

Call daddy if you need anything, he said to me as I got out the car.

K daddy love you, I said while planting a kiss on his cheek.

Love you to stink, he said before pulling off.

I climbed the front steps, and stuck my key in the door, I was instantly hit with the smell of sweet potatoes. I made my way thru the house into the kitchen, I was happy as hell I didn't see any sign of troy.

Hey ma, I said in a low tone, because I didn't know what type of mood she was in today.

Hey, she said dryly without even looking up from the food.

Since you're here I need to run to the store, she said grabbing her things, and leaving.

I peeped at the food, good thing every item she was cooking, you didn't have to stand over it, so I turned to leave out the kitchen when the house phone rung.

Hello, I answered.

Try not to make too much noise, Troy's upstairs sleeping, she said before hanging up in my face.

My whole body froze, why do she insist on leaving me here with him. Maybe he won't wake up till she comes back, I thought till I heard a toilet flush. I heard his footsteps leading down the hall to the steps. My heart begins to pound, as I made my way to the front door, I was halfway on the porch when he snatched me back in.

Hustla:

I was sitting outside Money's baby mama house, watching her boyfriend for him. So far this nigga ain't done shit, to me it seems like he just sit around and mooch off Nyla. Last night while she left, this nigga brought another bitch over, they were by themselves for a minute too. Earlier today I saw money drop Yotti fine ass off, soon after Nyla left alone, I knew that nigga was still in there so I called money.

Yo, he answered on the second ring.

ayee wea you at, I asked him.

Around the way was up, he said.

Babymoms just left, with that nigga in the house, I told him.

Where the fuck my daughter at, he asked getting louder.

In the house, I said.

Get your ass in there, don't let him see you, and don't let him hurt my stink, he said before hanging up.

I hopped out the car, jogging the two houses down to get to theirs. I walked on the side of their neighbor's house and climbed the fence to their backyard. I peeped in the living room window but didn't see nobody, the whole downstairs was empty. I checked the front door, but it was locked, I walked around to the back, and pushed the kitchen window, and it opened. I climbed thru, pulled out my gun, and quietly walked thru the downstairs, checking every room. I unlocked the front door as I quietly crept up the stairs, all the doors where open, and lights were off except for one room, I walked towards the room when I heard the front door quietly close. I spun around aiming my gun at the front door only to see Money.

Where the fuck they at, he whispered coming up the steps with his gun in his hands.

I pointed towards the closed door, when we got close to the door you could hear muffled screams.

Yotti:

My throat hurt so bad from tryna scream with this tape over my mouth, troy sick ass had me tied to my bed. Tears rolled down my eyes, as I silently prayed that my mama would hurry back.

You know how long I been waiting to feel inside of you, he said as he begins to rub my thigh with one hand and pulling his short fat dick out with the other. Tears begin to roll down my face harder, I wanted to throw up. He reached down and pulled my shorts off; I begin to scream hard and as loud as the tape would let me. I was still a virgin, and I refuse to lose it this way, and by him.

Shut up, he said as he reached down to grab my panties.

Boom

I heard a loud bump, but I couldn't see cause of the way I was sitting.

How the fuck you get in my house, troy said standing up, not even bothering to put his dick up.

Fuck you thought you was doing with that, a familiar voice said, before hitting troy with the butt of his gun several times.

Daddy, I said, but it was muffled because of the tape.

I felt somebody untie my hands, as daddy beat the shit out of troy. As soon as my hands were free, I ripped the tape off my mouth and ran to daddy.

Daddy, I screamed out, it was like he was stuck just beating Troy's ass, but when I called his name, he snapped back into reality.

He wrapped his arms around me hugging me tight.

You alright stink, he asked me. I nodded my head.

Put sum pants on, and wait in the car, he said handing me the keys.

I did as he said and jetted downstairs, the minute I hit the bottom step I smelled something burning, I just cut the whole stove off, I couldn't be in this house another minute. I waited in the car like daddy said, when the boy he was with came out the house jogging up the street to a black-on-black car parked two houses down, he hoped in the car pulling it around to the back yard. I watched out the window, as they carried tied up troy out to the car putting him in the trunk. The boy got in the car and pulled off, as daddy went inside the house thru the back door. He was in there for about 10 mins when I saw mama pulling up. Her face scrunched up when she saw daddy's car. She got out grabbed a few bags, and walked past me into the house, I followed right behind her.

What the fuck is that smell, she asked when she walked in.

She walked to the kitchen, I looked up the steps, and daddy looked like he was cleaning off something.

Yatise! My mother yelled at the top of her lungs from the kitchen.

Yes ma, I said walking into the kitchen.

I thought I told you to watch the food, what the fuck were you doing that you burnt the sweet potatoes, she yelled getting in my face.

Nyla! I need to talk to you for a minute, my daddy said from the doorway.

What do you want, and why are you here? she asked sounding frustrated.

Stink go wait in the car, he said looking at me.

For what she's not leaving with you, if you don't want her in our conversation she can wait in her room, my mother said putting her hand on her hip.

You are so pathetic Nyla it's sad, you think it’s okay to leave your boyfriend here with her, he asked her.

What! Yatise is old enough to take care of herself, and Troy don't be stutting her, what would he want with her, she said laughing.

But my daddy was serious, next thing I know my daddy had my mama pinned against the wall by her neck, he did it so fast she didn't even see it coming.

I just walked in on this nigga tryna rape my daughter, and you think it’s funny, he said tighting his grip on her neck.

She begins to gasp tryna get air, my daddy let her go causing her to fall to the ground.

Let's go Yatise, he said looking at me.

I followed behind him as we heard my mama say something.

Where is troy, she asked.

My daddy kept walking until he noticed I stopped. I walked back to my mother who was still tryna catch her breath.

I try my hardest to respect you, and do as you ask, I make good grades, and never fail to help you cook or clean, I take your nagging and constant down talk about my daddy all to respect you, I've let u hit, smack, and punish me for no reason at all, and not one time did I run and tell anybody.

I sat back and allowed your boyfriend to look at me any kind of way, say anything to me, and not once told because I didn't want him to slit your throat like he said he would.

I've taken a lot from you, my daddy just told you that Troy tried to rape me and all you're worried about is his were about. you never even wanted me, you wanted to keep my daddy around, but when u realized having me wasn't going to keep him around you started to mistreat me, because I looked like him, I laughed as tears streaked my face.

I remember times you would beat my ass because you said I talked about them too much, I hope you find happiness, because I don't ever want to see your pathetic face again, I yelled before storming out the house, with daddy behind me.

CHAPTER EIEGHT

Money:

Wake yo bitch ass up, I said as I splashed hot water on Troy.

I had him tied facedown, legs apart on a pool table, butt ass naked.

Aghh what the fuck man, he yelled tryna wiggle his hand around in the rope.

Shut up bitch, I said as I positioned myself in front of him with the pool stick.

Hustla tossed me a ball, I put it on the table in front of his face.

So did you honestly think you was gone get away with tryna rape my daughter, I said not really looking for an answer. He opened his mouth to speak, but as soon as the first sound left his mouth, I hit the ball hard with the pool stick, causing it to hit his mouth, blood gushed out.

Please man it wasn't what you think, she came on to me, she teased me, he cried out.

If he knew better, he would shut the fuck up, every time he talked it made me madder and madder.

Did I ask you to talk huh, I asked as I begin to hit every ball that belonged to the pool table at his face.

When I was finishing his face had cuts, and blood gushing from everywhere, but I still wasn't satisfied. I took the pool stick, and beat the shit out of him with it till it broke on his back.

You put yo dirty ass hands on my daughter, you threatened her, I said while walking to the back.

I came back out with my dog muffins, you gone tie my fucking stink up, I said talking to no one in particular, I was just venting. I put muffins on the pool table and sat down in front of it so troy could see my face. Muffins licked around on parts of his body, before finding Troy's balls.

Cum on man get this dog, he is licking my shit man, he cried out.

So what bitch, you wanna act like a pussy, you gone get fucked like one, I said leaning directly in his face.

Hell, naw I can't watch that shit, hustla said turning away.

I looked at muffins, who had begun to lick around Troy's ass, while hunching his thigh.

Hump muffins, hump, I said as muffins scooted up some, causing his pink part to poke at Troy's ass cheeks, Troy squeezed his butt hard as he begged me to get the dog.

I leaned closer to his face. Did you stop when my daughter begged you, this my fuckin city nigga, everybody knows not to fuck with me, but your dumb ass, I said while laughing, and putting gloves on.

I'm tired of playing with you, I said as I spreadded his ass cheeks letting muffins find his way in. I stepped back as troy hollered from the pain, and muffins howled from the pleasure. Muffins was going so hard it started to smell like shit.

Let's go, muffins will be mad if he don't catch his nut, I told hustla as we left the warehouse laughing.

Yotti:

After daddy dropped me off at aunt Chell's, I had to calm myself down. I can't believe I was so close to getting raped by troy, thank god that daddy was there. After getting myself together Kayla, and MyMy talked me into going out to eat with them.

So it's the summer what's our plans, Kayla asked as she looked over the menu.

I was about to say something when her phone interrupted me.

Hello, she answered,

Yeah we're in the back, she said.

Right here papi, she said slightly waving her hand.

I turned to see who she was talking to, and almost shited a brick when I saw three dudes heading our way.

I kicked her foot under the table, ouch, she quietly yelled, bitch you didn't tell me they were coming, I whispered. But they made it to our table before she could respond.

Hey papi, Kayla said, standing up hugging the dark skin dude with the fade. He was tall, with plump pink lips.

Was gud lady, he said back to her.

This is Yotti, and MyMy, she said pointing to us.

And this is Kai, Dee, and Tae, she said pointing at the boys.

Hey, MyMy, and I said at the same time.

My attention was on Dee, he looked better than he sounded on the phone, He was tall with smooth chocolate skin, and pretty white teeth. He had long dreads, and a mustache. He sat down beside me, as Kayla got out to let Tae in the booth beside MyMy.

What happened to you calling me, Dee asked once everybody was settled in.

Um I broke my phone, I just got a new one today, I said while holding my phone up that still had the plastic on it.

He grabbed my phone out my hand, swiped his finger across to unlock it, and dialed a number. His phone started to ring, my number flashed across his screen. He locked my number in his phone and stood up.

Come on let's sit over there, he said pointing to an empty table, I got up and followed him.

I enjoyed his company, before we left the restaurant, Kayla told them to come over when aunt Chell leave for work, the agreed, and we left.

CHAPTER NINE

Yotti:

I sat on the front porch waiting for Mell to come get me, my daddy now has custody of me. With Melanie being one of the best attorney's it didn't take much to prove how unfit my mother was. I haven't heard from my mama in six months, she hasn't called me and I'm damn sure not calling her. I stood up as I saw Mell pull into the driveway, I locked the front door, and got in the car as she pulled off. My birthday was in a couple of days, and I needed a dress. After several hours of shopping, I finally found a dress that daddy would approve of. We stopped to eat then headed home. Daddy haven't made it home yet, Mell went in her office to do some work, I was upstairs hanging my dress when my phone rung.

Hey baby, I sang into the phone.

Was up ma what you doing? Dee asked me.

Dee and I have been talking for six months but made our relationship official two months ago.

Nothing just got back in, what you doing? I asked him.

Chilln just left school, are you going over your auntie's this weekend, he asked.

I don't know, I know you didn't forget about my birthday, I said to him.

Of course not, that's why you need to go over yo auntie's, he said.

Um when daddy comes in, I will see if he could drop me off, but ima need you to take me to the nail shop in the morning, I told him.

You know I got you ma, just call me when you get there aight, he said.

I said OK and we hung up.

Later that night daddy dropped me off at Kayla's, we were getting dressed to go to a party with Dee, and Kai.

So, you know Donna supposed to be there, Kayla said as she flat ironed my hair.

And if tha bitch jump, then its whatever cause I'm wit it, I told her

Donna is some girl that goes to school with Kayla, and they couldn't get along for shit. I love my cousin a bitch couldn't touch her with a 50ft pole without me walking 50ft to smack that bitch.

Two hours later we were pulling up at the party and it was asshole. We went inside, there was a guy serving drinks, we walked to the bar to get a drink.

What you want ma, Dee asked me.

I shrugged my shoulders, I've never drunk before so I didn't know what to order, Kayla made a suggestion for me. We got our drinks and was headed to the back when some light skin skinny girl stopped Dee.

Hey baby what happened to you last night, she asked not giving a fuck if I was standing there or not.

He looked at her like she was crazy, wrong move shawty, I'm wit my gal, he said while placing his hand on my lower back brushing past her.

That's what I loved about Dee rather he fucks off or not, he never let that shit affect me, and when I'm in his presence he put his hoes in their place. After dancing for a little while Dee, and Kai left to go handle something. Kayla and I went to get another drink when I had the urge to pee. After coming out of the bathroom we bumped into Donna and two other girls.

Stuck up bitch, Donna slurred as she bumped Kayla.

Are you mad or naw?, Kayla asked her.

Donna starred at her before saying, you're lucky I don't wanna fuck up my friend's house, or I would of been whooped your ass.

Outside is wide open, Kayla calmly said.

Let's go then bitch, Donna said walking past Kayla with her two do girls behind her. There was three against two, although Kayla is older I'm bigger than her so nine times out of ten two were gonna try to gang me. Kayla didn't even let Donna get all the way out the door before she snatched her and start beating her. I grabbed the girl that was closest to me, pulled her shirt over her head and start beating her.

Get the fuck off my sister hoe, the other girl yelled running towards us.

I pushed the girl I had pinned down in front of me so her sister couldn't get to me, I begin to swing at the bigger sister with my right hand, as I held the Lil sister down with my left hand. It was working till the Lil sister came completely out of her shirt. Fuck now I gotta fight both these bitches head up, I thought fuck it let's go. They both rushed me at the same time, I ran head up into the first one, grabbing her hair as the other one pulled my hair from the back.

Get off my cuzin, I heard Kayla yell before I felt a hard tug, then my hair was free, I got on top of gal and blacked out.

CHAPTER TEN

Money:

Me and hustla, was on the way to a party to drop a package off to some of my boys. It was a big ass crowd surrounding two fights.

Hell naw, they gotta get this shit later, this fight gone run the block hot, I said about to pull off, when a nigga name slim stopped my truck.

Yo money man, that's yo daughter and niece fighting, he said between breaths.

I hopped out the truck pushing my way thru the crowd, when I got there Yotti was sitting on top of one girl beating the shit out of her, and Kayla had the other girl slanging her ass from left to right. My girls were doing so good I didn't wanna stop them, but they were fucking up my money.

Yotti:

I felt somebody lifting me up in the air and pushing me into a truck. Wait whose truck is this Dee has a charger, I turned around.

Daddy! what are you doing here, and where is Kayla, I asked turning to look in the backseat.

She was in the back tryna catch her breath, there was a boy beside her, but I turned my attention back to daddy who was yelling at me.

This my hood Lil girl, the question is what tha fuck y'all doing here, he snapped on the both of us.

I asked her to go with me Uncle Maurice, these girls said they were gone gang me, Kayla said taking the blame off me.

He took a deep breath, y'all did good by the way, he said

When we got back to auntie's I hopped straight in the shower. When I got out Dell was sitting on my bed smoking a blunt.

Where were you tonight, I asked him as I begin to lotion my body.

I told you I was going to handle something, what the fuck happened, he asked turning his attention to me.

I don't wanna talk about it, my head hurts, I said while putting a shirt and shorts on, and climbing in the bed.

He got up put the blunt out, went to shut the door and lock it. He walked to the bed stripping down to his gym shorts and climbed in the bed. He wrapped his arm around me and pulled me close to him, I dozed off in his arms.

The next morning, I woke up, and Dell was gone, I sucked my teeth, and rolled over to grab my phone, he sent me a text.

Dell: morning beautiful I had a run to make, I should be back by the time you're dressed, I got chu birthday girl.

A smiled spread across my face, I jumped up to shower, and get dressed, once I was finished, I shot him a text saying I'm ready.

An hour later, I was at the nail shop getting a pedicure, and manicure. The lady kept getting smart because Dell flirted with me the whole time. After we left, we went out to eat. Everything was going well until I ran into Mell and daddy.

What the fuck you doing here, and who is he, my daddy said pointing to Dell.

Um hi daddy, this is my friend Dell, Dell that's my daddy Money, and my mama Melanie, I said sounding nerves as hell.

Hey how y'all doing, Dell spoke to them.

Who you here with?, my daddy asked me completely ignoring Dell.

I'm with him daddy, I was just getting a Mani, and Pedi, that's all, I said.

If that's all why the fuck you in a restaurant, he said making it a big deal.

They were probably hungry Maurice, you're over exaggerating, cut her some slack she is the birthday girl, Mell spoke up.

Whatever, my daddy said waving her off, how old you is, he said looking at Dell

16, Dell stated.

You know my daughter's only 14, he asked like our age difference was an issue.

Actually I'm 15 now daddy, I stated before he shot me the death glare.

Maurice really! Mell said getting frustrated.

What! Daddy said as if he didn't say anything wrong, well since you riden around with this nigga I hope he treated you to everything, I raised you not to settle for less, he said.

He did daddy, were just friends stop making it an issue, I said getting frustrated.

Let's go Maurice, Yotti you know what to do and what not to do, Mell said stopping my daddy from saying anything else, and they left.

Later that night daddy had got me a limo for my party. We pulled up and to my surprise it was epic, there were people from my school, and Kayla's. Daddy had rented out the ball room of a hotel, and Mell, aunt Chell, and Aunt Sonya, had it decorated, fit for a princess. I walked around looking for Dell, I said hi to everybody who stopped to wish me a happy birthday, I saw Dell by the entrance talking to daddy. I rolled my eyes cuz I can only imagine what daddy was saying to him.

Daddy are you scaring my date, I asked walking up to them, planting a kiss on daddy's face.

Naw I was just letting him know that if he hurt my daughter, ima chop his limbs off and mail em to his mama piece by piece, daddy said with a chuckle, but I knew he was serious as hell.

Thanks, daddy, for keeping him company, but I got it from here, I said while pulling Dell away.

You look good girl, Dell said while sliding his hand over my ass.

I quickly pushed it up to my lower back, I looked back at daddy to see if he saw, but Mell had him occupied.

Everybody was having fun I think everybody was a Lil tipsy tho, because someone spiked the punch, we were so turnt, the people at the hotel put us out. I went home showered and waited up for Dell to call but he never did.

CHAPTER ELEVEN

Dell(Dee):

Wat up, wat up, I said answering the phone for my nigga snake.

Was up my nigga? wats going on, he asked.

Errthing green on my end what about yours's, I asked.

Shit gravy got that Lil piece of info for you, he said sounding more serious.

Aight so wea DA spot, I asked him.

We met up at one of his freaks houses.

I got some good news, and better news, which one you want first, he asked while taking a blunt from behind his ear firing it up.

Give me the good, I said taking tha blunt from him hitting it.

I know who robbed yo spot a few days ago, he said.

Who! I asked feeling myself get mad all over again.

Hustla, he said hitting the blunt.

Hustla, hustla I tossed his name around my head tryna figure out wea I know him from, then it clicked.

You talm bout one of money guys, the one that drive the black Magnum, I asked.

He nodded his head, as he passed the blunt.

What's the better news, I asked.

I got an address, he said sliding a piece of paper to me.

I looked at it, stood up handed him the blunt, and hit him up before I left.

Appreciate that my nigga, stay in touch, I told him as I walked out the door.

Ain't this some bullshit, how crazy is it that my spot just got robbed by my girlfriend's daddy people. I'm far from a hoe, somebody gotta pay, but I'm not stupid either. Money is ahead of my time and got niggas on his payroll that can touch you from a distance. But fuck all that I'm far from pussy, somebody gotta pay.

Yotti:

Its been a year, and everything was cool until school started back two weeks ago. Daddy got me transferred to Kayla, Dell, and Kai's school, and come to find out the little skinny girl Dell and I had ran into, a while back at the party, he's fucking her, so were not on speaking terms right now. Yesterday the skinny girl Tiffany tried to embarrass me, But today I wasn't in a good mood, I want the bitch to buck. I sat in third block waiting for the bell to ring, I was hungry as hell. I'm tired of going back and fourth with texting Dell, and honestly I didn't care to see him today.

Yotti, I heard somebody whisper my name.

It was one of my classmates Lola, she just moved here. She's only been here a week, and she flocked to me instantly.

The bell rung, I quickly grabbed my stuff, I was ready to eat. Lola walked up to me as I was walking out the door.

Hey girl, she said walking beside me.

Was up, I said stopping at my locker to put my books up.

Nothing do you mind if I eat lunch with you today, she asked.

I laughed, of course Lola you know your cool, I told her as we begin walking towards MyMy locker.

Hey I have to use the bathroom, Lola said walking towards the bathroom.

Go ahead we'll find a table, MyMy told her.

We walked in the cafeteria, and got in the snack line. Um can I get a wing basket, naked fried hard, I told the lunch lady, can you make that two please, MyMy added.

MyMy:

The lunch lady gave us our food, we grabbed a drink, paid for our food and was about to walk out the line when tiffany bumped Yotti, sending her wings, and fries flying in the air.

Watch were your going bit-- she barely got out before Yotti sent her cold drink flying to the back of Tiffany's head. She pushed Tiffany into the back wall of the snack line, and started hitting her. Yotti hands we're swinging so fast Tiffany didn't know what to do. Then the other three girls she was with jumped in. I dropped my food snatching the first one off her, we started rumbling but she was no match for me.

Kayla:

I was sitting in the gym, when a fight broke out next door in the cafeteria. Everybody, started to Leave out the gym to go watch but I wasn't in the mood for all that.

Yo Kayla, they ganging yo cousin, a boy named rob said.

I jumped up running full speed to the cafeteria, pushing anybody that got in my way, When I got there security had MyMy, the two girls that ran wit tiff, and that new girl Lola Yotti started hanging with pinned against the wall. Another security was tryna break Yotti up, she was sitting on tiffany, and another girl had Yotti hair, the security was tryna get the girl to let her hair go. I walked around the security, snatched her so hard her fingers slipped right thru Yotti hair. Yotti looked up, and when I saw her face I freaked out, I still had the girl by her hair, so I started hitting her. I didn't give a fuck wea I hit her at nose, mouth, eye, jaw, ear I didn't give a fuck. My cousin had a black eye I was determined to give these hoe's one if they didn't already have one. Blood started popping up as I continued to hit her, until security snatched me off her taking me to the office with everybody else.

Yotti:

I stormed out the office mad as hell, they wouldn't even let us leave together we had to leave one by one.

Baby you alright, dell asked walking up to me.

Don't touch me dell, I said without looking at him.

Baby don't, he said lifting my face to his but stopped when he seen my eye.

What happened yatise, I heard my daddy from behind.

I was scared to turn around because I know he gone go off about my eye.

I turned around, and just like I thought he started panicking like it was the end of the world.

What happened to yo eye stink, who did that to daddy baby, awww damn stink, he said pacing back and forth in font of the office.

Daddy it’s just a black eye it will heal, I told him.

But you my baby, who the fuck would wanna put they hands on my baby, you too pretty for that, he said frustrated.

Daddy I'm not 5, I'm tired I wanna lay down, can you please go get Kayla so we can go.

He turned and walked in the office, I turned to Dell.

Look dell you got to much going on for me I think I need my space, I said as daddy walked out with Kayla, and MyMy.

On our way out the school we ran into Lola's mama.

Oh my goodness baby what happed to your eye, she said lifting my head up so she could examine it.

Ugh I got jumped, tell Lola I said thanks, and sorry Ms Douglas for getting her in trouble, I said to her mother

You're fine baby, the way your eye look she would have been in trouble if she didn't jump in, she said laughing.

I laughed to, it was good seeing you, I said walking off.

You to baby stay out of trouble, she said.

We all climbed in the truck, he dropped us off at the house, and left.

CHAPTER TWELEVE

Yotti:

They suspended everybody for two weeks, and those two weeks flew by. Now I'm suspended again, because when we got back from our first suspension, the minute i laid eyes on Tiffany I beat her ass. I beat her so bad the ambulance had to come. Daddy didn't raise no hoe, he kept me and Mell up long nights hitting them punching bags, every time he take his weekly trip to the gun range, he drag me right with him. I'm grateful for my parents, not only do the make sure I'm book smart, but daddy also make sure I'm street smart too. He always says, you my daughter so you're already a target for people to come up, don't let a bitch catch you slipping, and never Fall weak to a nigga. My daddy has never led my wrong so everything he tell me I take it to heart. He told me never go to sleep without my pistol, cause when you're sleep you're at your weakest. Don't depend on nobody, not even yo circle cause ain't nobody got you like you got you. I was snapped out of my thoughts, when Mell asked me a question.

What you thinking about, she asked as she typed information in her computer.

Since I was suspended, I was at the office with Mell, I loved coming to the office with her. She's the one who inspired me to become a lawyer.

Nothing, I'm kind of hungry, I told her.

Well we have enough time, to stop and get something to eat before my Dr. Appt. She said while standing up.

I laughed cuz I wasn't use to seeing her that big.

What's funny, she said walking around her desk playfully hitting me in the head with a folder.

Ima go run this to Mitchel, then we can leave, she said walking out her office.

We ate before heading to the doctors office. After checking on my baby brother, we went home. I was sitting in the den eating ice cream, when somebody knocked on the door.

Yotti, I'm in the bathroom can you get that, Mell yelled from downstairs.

I jogged down stairs to open the door for an older women, Who kind of resembled mell. But I've never heard Mell talk about her family, except for her sister. The woman looked down at me, and by the way she held her nose up, you could tell she was stuck up.

Hello how may I help you, I asked after getting tired of the stare down.

Does Melanie live here, she asked looking around me into the house.

May I ask who wants to know, I asked her. Shit daddy taught me not to give up information.

Yotti whose at the door, Mell asked coming out of her room towards us.

What are you doing here Melissa, Mell asked the woman.

How rude, are you going to at least invite me in, she asked her.

Mell sighed, Yotti can you brew me some tea please.

I turned to head to the kitchen, as Mell invited the woman in. They went straight to the living room, so I could hear there whole conversation.

You have a beautiful home Melanie, the women spoke.

Thanks Melissa, but what are you doing here, Mell asked the woman again.

Can we not have a mother, and daughter conversation, can we not argue for once, the woman spoke.

Mell laughed, OK I don't know what kind of game your playing, but I'll play along.

Its not a game, but when is the baby due, Melissa asked her.

I brought Mell her tea, and made it just the way she liked it.

I'm sorry did you want some tea Mrs.

Mrs Melissa, the woman corrected me.

I'm sorry Mrs Melissa, I asked.

No sweetie I'm fine, and who are you, she asked.

Melissa this is my daughter Yotti, Yotti this is my mother Melissa, Mell said introducing us.

She laughed, never knew you had a daughter.

Well its alot you don't know about me, since you could care less if you're apart of my life or not, Mell shot at her.

The front door opened drawing all our attention.

Baby, my daddy yelled from the front door.

In the living room, she called out.

Hey daddy, I said as I hugged, and kissed him.

Wasup, stink, go get daddy something to drink, he said as he walked towards Mell.

Was up ma, my daddy said to Mell.

Hey daddy, she said back as they kissed.

Mrs Melissa literally rolled her eyes.

How you doing Mrs Nelson, my daddy spoke to Melissa, but she didn't speak back.

Mell laughed, baby could you give us a minute please.

My daddy nodded his head, and walked off to the kitchen with me.

OK Melissa let's cut the bullshit what is this visit about, Mell said sounding pissed off.

Well I can see you're in a bad mood, but as you know Monica, and Dominic, has been staying with us, and with those twins of Dominic's running around, the house has become to crowded, and you have plenty of space here.

Mell laughed hard, before Melissa could even finish what she was saying.

Let me get this straight, first you worshipped the ground Dominic walked on, you always through up in my face how she was gone be a successful doctor, and how pretty she was, and how proud she made you, let's not forget she's not even your real daughter, you down talked me because I married a drug dealer, as you would call it, you talked about how stupid I was, and how he was gone fuck me over, need I remind you he's the one that put me through college not you. I don't hear from you in years, you show up at my doorstep out the blue, and then you disrespect my husband by not speaking back. This his house he don't have to speak to you, and you gone have the nerve to not speak to my husband, and now you wanna ask for favors. I don't even like Dominic, so you can take that dumb ass suggestion, and get the hell out of my house, Mell snapped on her.

I looked over at my daddy who was silently laughing.

Well, I see you haven't changed a bit, still disrespecting yo mama, with your ghetto ass, Melissa said heading towards the door.

Whatever, you didn't start acting boogie, till you married Bill's stuck-up ass, so you can take that fake ass accent on somewhere, Cuz I get my ghettoness from you, Mell said before closing the door.

I couldn't help but to laugh, me and daddy was in the kitchen dying laughing.

Her moms don't like me foreal, daddy said still laughing.

Nobody likes you; my granny doesn't like you either, I said referring to my mama's mama.

While you sitting over there laughing, can you go to the store to get me some ice cream, Mell asked daddy walking into the kitchen.

Its ice cream in the freezer, he said.

I don't want that kind, I want peanut butter, she said to him.

He got up and left to go to the store, I got up to answer my phone.

Was up Lola's baby, I said answering the phone for Lola.

Hey, can you have company, she asked.

Yeap, I responded

OK my mama is bringing me over, she said before hanging up.

When Lola got there, we decided to go swimming since it was so hot, Mell got her big ass in the pool, and daddy grilled us some burgers. I swear I lov g here with them.

CHAPTER THIRTEEN

I sat my 4-month-old brother down in his crib. Melanie had him on August 5, 2005, one day after my birthday. She named him Maurice Jr after my daddy, but daddy calls him boss. I went the next door over to my room and took a shower. After I got out, I talked on the phone to Dell till I fell asleep.

Pow, pow, pow,

I jumped out my sleep, did I just here gun shots, I thought. I jumped out of bed grabbing my 22, I crept out my room to my brothers, but he was still sleep. I heard moving downstairs, so I quietly followed the sound. My heart was pounding, and I was scared as shit, but my family was in danger. I don't know about you, but I was willing to ride and die for mine. I saw a shadow sprint past the living room into the kitchen, I followed them. I caught them climbing out the kitchen window, I aimed my gun, that's when I noticed a tattoo, one that I knew all too well. Shoot Yotti shoot, I told myself, but I couldn't, and just like that they were gone. I ran as fast as I could thru the house till I got to daddy's room, the door was half open, I pushed it open, and my heart immediately dropped to the floor, tears rolled down my face, I couldn't move, I couldn't speak, but I had to see if they were OK. I walked over to my daddy who held Mell's lifeless body in his arms. She had a hole in the middle of her forehead. I've never seen daddy cry until now, I reached over to grab daddy's arm that's when I noticed he had a hole in his chest.

They took her baby girl, they took my world from me, he said between sobs, and coughs.

Daddy we have to get help, I said reaching for the phone, but he stopped me.

Daddy please I've already lost Mell, I can't lose you too, I said through tears.

I can't cough, I can't live with myself knowing she died cause of me, I'm already gone stink, but you gotta be strong for your brother, promise me no matter what you will always have your brother back, he said between cough's,

I promise daddy, I said to him.

Go look in the safe and take everything out, the code is your birthday, make sure you guard those papers with your life, he said

I got up and did as he said I took a duffle bag, and put all the money that would fit inside one, and grabbed another one putting the rest of the money, and the paperwork inside. I ran back to daddy who was now slumped over with his eyes closed.

Daddy please daddy please get up, I said pulling him into my lap.

He coughed then said I love you and yo brothers, you'll be straight for the rest of your life. Never forget anything I've ever taught you. He smiled, prettiest girl in the world, Jr. cough. Cough, cough, yo brother... Yo brother.... Detroit. Was all he said before coughing uncontrollably, then taking his last breath in front of me.

Noooo daddy please get up, daddy I need you, daddy please, I cried and begged for him to come back to me, but he was gone.

A loud knock at the door snapped me out of it.

Police open up, they yelled

I got up and drugged the two big heavy duffle bags upstairs stuffing them in the back of my closet, before opening the door. After answering a ton of questions, the police finally let us leave with aunt Chell. The day of the funeral I was sick to my stomach, I couldn't eat or sleep, I felt so empty. Two weeks after the funeral, we were settled in at aunt Chell's. I was lying in bed, but got up to check on my brother. I walked in his room, auntie was sitting in a rocking chair holding him, watching him as he slept. I walked in and sat Indian style in front of her.

She looked at me then closed her eyes, you have eyes just like him, she said as a tear rolled down her face.

I know it's hard to look at myself right now, I said to her.

We sat there in silence, in our own thoughts when my mind drifted off to the last conversation I had with daddy.

I love you and yo brothers, yo brotha Detroit, what did he mean by that.

Hey auntie did my daddy have any kids besides us, I asked her.

Not that I know of why, she asked.

Just asking, I said.

She got up to lay the baby down, I have to work in a Lil bit, when Kayla come in y'all clean up my house, and cook that chicken I took out, she said heading out the room.

OK auntie, I said before heading to my own room.

I laid down, and begin to scroll down my timeline on insta, when I ran across a picture of Tiffany and Dell. My blood begins to boil immediately, on some real shit I'm through with him. He been on some fuck shit lately, he's been real disrespectful ever since my daddy died, I picked up the phone and called him.

Watup girl, he answered on the third ring.

Where are you, I asked really losing interest in him.

Riding round, he responded.

Oh, why is there pictures of you and Tiff on insta, I asked him

That's old girl, he lied.

She just posted it this morning, I said.

But we took tha picture a long time ago, he lied again.

I know that pictures not old because your shirt in the picture is new, you know what, fuck you Dell, I said before hanging up.

CHAPTER FOURTEEN

Its been a week since I broke up with Dell, and he blows my phone up daily non stop. I was waiting on Kayla to pull up, she went to get Lola, and MyMy so we could go to the mall. I slipped boss shoe back on when I heard her blowing, we hopped in the car and pulled off. When we got to the mall I mostly shopped for boss, I've learned to put him before me, my daddy asked me to look out for him so that's what I do. After shopping we headed to the food court, I held boss on my hip as we passed a group of boys.

Excuse me, one of them stopped me.

I turned around, and that nigga was cute as hell. He had a honey colored skin tone, with thick eyebrows, and nice plump lips. He was tall and muscular, as if he played football. his arms were covered in tattoos. He rocked a high top fade with a taper, and his hair was semi curly.

hi, I said as I put boss on my opposite hip.

You look familiar, don't I know you, he asked.

I laughed why do niggas gotta use the same line, naw you don't know me, I said as I turned to walk of,

He gently grabbed my arm, I do know you what's you name, he asked.

You may know of me but I doubt you know me, I said moving my hand and walking off.

I'm sorry about yo daddy, he said.

I stopped in my tracks, how do you know my daddy, I said walking closer to him.

Were going to sit over there, Kayla said pointing to an empty table as MyMy grabbed boss out my arms.

I turned my attention back to the dude, how do you know my daddy, I asked him again.

Come on, he said grabbing my hand leading me to the table where Kayla them were.

Yo daddy was my God daddy, he use to run with my daddy ceaser, he said as we sat down.

I remember uncle ceaser, but I don't remember you, I said.

Remember about a year or two ago y'all got the fighting on lewis at a party, he said pointing at me and Kayla.

The dude that was in the back, Kayla spoke up.

He nodded his head, see we on the same team baby girl, now can I get your number, he said looking at me.

I laughed, you don't even know my name yet.

I know yo name Yotti, yo daddy talked about you all the time, he said with a smile showing a bottom grill.

You can give me your number, I said.

He sucked his teeth, you better call me to girl.

He put his number in my phone and left.

Wait what's your name, I called out to him.

Hustla.

The next day flew by, I wanted to call hustla so bad but I didn't wanna seem desperate so I didn't call. I was sitting on the floor playing with boss when my phone rung. I didn't recognize the number so I didn't answer, but I wanted to know who it was so I called back.

Hello, a male voice said.

Did someone call this number, I asked.

Yea but you should've called me when you got home from the mall, he said.

I laughed, how you get my number.

I been having it, what you don't won't me to have it, he asked.

I didn't say that, I was just wondering how you got it, I said.

Um what you doing, can I come see you, he asked.

Yes you can come see me, I will text you the address, I told him.

Where you, over yo aunties, I know where its at, he said.

OK I'll see you in a few, I said before hanging up.

I jumped up to freshen up, and straighten up. I heard voices downstairs, but I thought I was the only one home. I went downstairs, and the first person I saw was Dell. Why the fuck is he here, he don't have to come every time Kai come. I turned to walk back upstairs when he stopped me.

Was up girl you can't return my calls, he asked.

No for what I don't fuck with you, I said.

Damn why you gotta be like that I apologized, he said.

But how many times are you gone have to because that gets old, why you just can't leave me alone, you now have the freedom to fuck tiff, and whoever else you want to, why you bothering me, I said getting frustrated.

He opened his mouth to say something, but I walked off cuz I heard my phone ringing.

Hello, I answered.

I'm outside, hustla said.

Dell:

I walked upstairs, as Yotti was walking to the back door.

Wea you going Yotti, I asked as I followed her outside.

When I got out there my body froze when I saw a black Magnum out there. I know this ain't who I think it is I thought. He got out the car and she went to hug him. This bitch is fucking my enemy.

What tha fuck y'all got going on, I said pissed off.

She looked at me, why the fuck you care.

What you mean why I care, you are fucking with the enemy now, I asked her.

So, the fuck what I don't give a fuck, you didn't give a fuck when you was fuckin Tiff, you didn't care that I didn't like that bitch you kept fucking her so you can miss me with all that, she said.

You got that I said.

I just hopped in my car and left she got me fucked up, Money ain't here to stop me now.

CHAPTER FIFTEEN

Hustla:

I give no fucks about seeing Dee, I know about him and her. Money couldn't stand that nigga that's why he paid me 10 racks plus whatever I find if I robbed a couple of his spots, I wasn't turning that down. Now he is going around telling everybody we enemies, and what he gone do when he see me. I laugh every time somebody tell me that, he is beefing with me I don't give a fuck about him. I done seen this nigga plenty of times, and he ain't done shit, real niggas don't talk they just do it.

I followed Yotti sexy ass to her room and sat down beside her on a love seat she had in her room.

What was that about, I asked.

That was just my ex, she responded

Why You all the way over there, I asked her while licking my lips.

She blushed while scooting closer to me a Lil bit. I gently grabbed her arm and pulled her closer.

You smell good, I told her while massaging her thigh.

Thanks, she said blushing harder.

I could feel her heart pounding, I make you nerves, I asked her.

No, she said giggling.

So, when you said yo ex, did you mean yo first, I asked her.

No, she simply said.

No, he wasn't yo first, orrr, she answered before I could finish.

I'm a virgin, she said.

Yotti:

We chilled in my room for bout a hour before Kayla came knocking on my door with boss. We decided to take boss to the park, since I had a couple of hours to spare before MyMy came over. Dell has been texting my phone non stop, Talm bout I'm a slut, I'm petty, and blah blah blah, then he gets mad cause I told him he just mad because hustla gone hit first, He was 380 hot, but so what you're hurting your own feelings keep calling and I don't wanna be bothered by you.

After we left the park, we went to get ice cream.

What's your real name, I asked him, I hated calling niggas by their street name. I felt like that was for the streets, and their homeboys and I'm neither.

He smiled, Hustla, he said showing of those pretty teeth.

I said real name, I said while giggling.

I'm just playing, its Langston, but only special people call me that, he said while licking his spoon. Lawd he look good, I thought.

So what you saying, I'm special, I asked him.

Hell yeah you special to me, I been wanting you every since the day I laid eyes on you, he said.

Why because I was in my panties, at first I couldn't remember where I knew him from, I mean I remembered him from the party, but I also remembered him before then, but couldn't figure out where until now, he was the same boy that helped daddy with troy.

He smirked, naw them panties wasn't that damn cute, he said causing both of us to laugh.

Hey babe what you doing here, we both turned around to look, it was some pretty brown skin girl.

I looked at him, and he looked shocked, um what's up girl, this my friend Yotti, Yotti that's Alicia.

His girlfriend, she spoke up correcting him.

I smiled hey, but the bitch cut me off.

Can I talk to you privately, she said ignoring me, talking to him.

I sucked my teeth tryna keep from going off on this bitch, cause she don't know me I will fuck her, and this dairy Queens up.

I'm going to the bathroom to change him, I said while grabbing boss, his bag, and brushed past her. We're leaving when I come from this bathroom rather he through talking to the bitch or not.

Hustla:

Who the fuck is she, Alicia semi yelled, as soon as Yotti left.

Calm the fuck down yo, I told you she's just a friend, I said.

A friend, she laughed, y'all must be the best of friends, you were so caught up in her you didn't even see me coming, she said sounding jealous.

Look Alicia I don't have time for what you tryna start, I told you she just a friend, and that's it, I said getting aggravated.

If she's just a friend how come you didn't introduce me as your girlfriend, so now I'm just Alicia, she snapped on me.

Mannnnn is you through, I said while massaging my temples.

I don't know why I said that knowing she hate that shit, she hated when I asked her, are you through? whenever we'd argue.

I'm ready to go, Yotti said while coming back grabbing her stuff.

We're talking right now sweetie, you can go on, Alicia said dismissing Yotti.

I looked at Yotti, who looked like she was finna snap, damn why Alicia gotta act like that.

Langston I'm ready to go now, Yotti said, more like demanded, as she walked off without waiting on a response.

I stood up and walked off behind her, only for Alicia to follow me.

Langston? Langston? who the fuck is she to be calling you Langston, his name is Hustla to you, she said turning towards Yotti.

Hol up hol up, Lee Lee you are tripping foreal, that girl ain't said two words to you for you to be acting the way you acting, I said getting tired of this bullshit.

Only female besides your family that should be calling you Langston is me, since when did you start telling side bitches your name, she snapped.

Yotti slammed the car door after buckling boos in, then turned towards Alicia.

Look bitch take yo old aggravating ass on, the man said we was just friends, so why is you doing the most, Yotti said walking closer to her.

I grabbed her by her waist, let's just go, I said pulling her towards the car.

Really, really, Alicia said walking around to my side, but I pulled off as soon as Yotti closed the door.

I looked over at her, I knew she was pissed, she had her arms folded and looked out the window the whole ride back.

She leaned to get out the car, but I stopped her, can I talk to you for a minute, I asked.

She looked back at boss who was knocked out, let me lay him down first, she said while getting out getting their stuff.

I watched her as she took him inside. It was something about Yotti that drove me crazy. Alicia is my girl, but some shit gets old. I do everything for Alicia,

I pay every bill in her house, pay car note, put gas in her car, make sure she keeps her hair and nails done. But she so unappreciative, its making me wanna walk away. We been messing around since I was 16, and she was 20, and I've never let her want for nothing, but that's where I fucked up at. Now she just sits around spend up my money and nag all day.

Yotti climbed her sexy ass back in the car, my mind immediately left Alicia, and was now on Yotti.

So why you didn't tell me you had a girlfriend, she asked.

I shrugged, to be honest, she never crossed my mind while I was with you, hell I didn't know why I didn't tell her, whenever I was with or talking to Yotti Licia was the last thing on my mind so I never brought it up.

What that got to do with you telling me you have a girl, you didn't forget you had a girlfriend, I don't give a damn who you're with you're not gonna forget that, she snapped.

You're right and I apologize, but I didn't wanna tell you because I liked you, and I know the minute I would of mentioned my girl you would have never answered the phone again, I said.

She sucked her teeth; you know we can't be no more than friends right.

CHAPTER SIXTEEN

Yotti:

It's been six months, Langston and I seem to grow closer every day. Things are different dating him then Dell, with Dell it was more like a middle school love being with Langston has put me on a whole nother level. Like I wear heels now, I've worn them a couple times before but now I wear them almost every day, I guess what I'm tryna say is Langston helped matured me. It doesn't even feel like boss is my brother anymore, that's my son, and you can't tell him Langston isn't Dada. When Langston and Alicia broke up, he went out and got an apartment, but of course auntie wasn't gone let us move in, but we might as well boss and I spend more time at Langston's then at home. I respect him so much; he makes sure he takes boss and I back and forth to school and makes sure we don't go without.

My 17th birthday is Monday, and boss 1st birthday is Tuesday. Me, auntie, and Kayla planned him a circus party, and when I say Langston went 0 too 100 for boss party stuff. He had a cotton candy machine, snow cone machine, candy bar with all types of candy, a merry go round, this nigga even ordered a dunking booth, he got a clown which I told him not to get them kids was scared as shit, it was funny tho. After everybody left, and we cleaned up, auntie agreed to watch boss for me so I could celebrate my birthday. I really wasn't in the mood to deal with a lot of people, so Langston and I went to the movies, and out to eat. We were having a good time till I saw Dell and Tiff being seated, seeing them didn't bother me, but her big belly did. I turned my attention back to Langston, who had butter from his shrimp above his lip.

You got something right here, I said while laughing and dabbing it with a napkin.

He smiled at me, you know you my heart right, he said serious.

I guess so, I shrugged and said.

Naw foreal Yatise I care about you a lot, you smart, ambitious, and determined. You got big dreams and I see you every day working to make em come true, and I salute you for that, you only 16 and you take care of your Lil brother like he yours and I respect you for that. That's why I never hesitate to make sure y'all got everything y'all need, I will never leave y'all hanging, and that's on my life, he said serious as hell.

I didn't know what to say, so I just leaned forward and kissed him, he had the softest lips, and the most passionate kiss I've ever felt.

I love you Langston, I blurted out, I was so caught up in the moment it slipped, but I meant it I loved Langston.

I love you to girl, he said with the biggest smile on his face.

After talking a little more, and finish eating we left, and went to Langston's, since I still had 3 hours before my curfew. Every time I walked in his house I felt at home, I guess because he let me decorate it. I slipped my shoes off and went to the bathroom, as he went straight for his stash. When I came out he was laid across the bed smoking, and playing the game. I crawled on the bed beside him, and took the dangling blunt from between his lips, and hit it, Hustla is the only person I will smoke with.

hustla

I got up and cut the game off, and walked to my closet to get one of her gifts. I grabbed the blunt from her and handed her the box.

You didn't have to give me anything, you've done enuff, she said examining the box.

Just open it baby, I told her while finishing off the blunt putting out the Roach.

She opened the box, as a smile spread across her face, what's this for she asked.

I didn't say nothing, I just nodded towards the bathroom, as she got up to get herself together. 30 mins later she walked out in the lingerie I got for her, I bit my bottom lip hard, Yotti was sexy as fuck hands down, and I don't even think she thru growing yet.

C'mere, I told her.

I watched her walk towards the bed, then crawled to me. My hands went straight to that ass, she leaned down and kissed me. I rolled her over to where she was on the bottom, and I was on top. I kissed her lips, then kissed her body, I put my hands inside her panties, she was wet as hell. I pulled em off, and spread her legs.

Wait Langston, I'm not ready yet, she said sounding like she was nervous about saying it.

I sighed, than rolled off her, I looked down at my stick, it was brick hard. She fixed her clothes, then looked at me.

What's wrong, she asked when she saw the look on my face.

I didn't say nothing I just grabbed her hand and put it on my throbbing dick.

I'm sorry baby, she said.

You good, I said walking to the bathroom.

CHAPTER SEVENTEEN

Yotti:

I woke up Monday morning with a smile, I said my prayers, and went to get my teeth, and face together. I heard my phone ringing, while coming out the bathroom.

Good morning Langston, I said answering the phone.

Happy birthday baby, he said.

Thank you, what time you coming, I said while blushing.

I'll be there in bout 30 mins, he said before we hung up.

I walked out my room, and the smell of breakfast hit my nose.

Happy birthday mami, I heard Kayla say when I walked past her room.

Thanks chica, I said as I went into my brothers room.

He was already up playing, he turned and saw me and smiled.

YaYa, he said as he ran up to me, I scooped him up and swung him around like I always did. I changed his diaper, washed him off, put his clothes on, and took him downstairs so auntie could feed him, while I got dressed. As I was spraying perfume on, I heard a knock at the back door, I turned to go open it but Kayla was already on her way, I got it, she said as she passed my door. I turned back to my vanity to put my lipstick on, when I saw Langston walk in my room looking, and smelling good as ever.

Damn you smell good, he said wrapping his arms around me kissing my neck.

Thanks you do to, I said while blushing.

He sat on the bed and fired up a blunt.

Aye baby go tell auntie come here right quick, he said taking a pull from the blunt.

I went downstairs, she was straighten up the mess she made, on the island sat sausage, eggs, potatoes, bacon, grits, and pancakes. Boss was stuffing his face with eggs.

Auntie Hustla want you, I said as I begin to fix hustla and I a plate, I knew he wasn't ready to eat yet, so I sat his plate in the the microwave.

Happy birthday Tisey bear, she said handing me a card.

Thanks auntie.

You're welcome, she said going upstairs.

I sat down beside boss and started eating, when Kayla came down.

You look cute boo, I told her.

Thanks love, so do you, she said.

After eating I went back upstairs, auntie and hustla were smoking and laughing. They've always been cool before me and him, he use to pick shit up from auntie, for daddy, so they always had a bond.

Auntie put the blunt out when I walked in with boss, and left the room. I sat boss down he immediately took off. I looked at the time, we had 15 mins to spare before it was time to leave for school. Hustla went downstairs to get his plate, and I opened my card, 500 dollars fell out, I read the card, and got up to put my money up, I sat the card on my dresser and went to think auntie again.

Langston picked boss up, as we headed out the door. Langston walked out first, when I got to the door my mouth dropped. there was a white Magnum, with a big purple bow on top.

Langston, I said as I turned to look at him, he was standing there holding my keys up smiling.

Go look, he said as he hit the unlock button.

I jetted to the car, and opened the door, the inside was all white with purple trimming, my name was engraved on the steering wheel, the head rest, and the glove compartment in purple. The front license plate read princess Yotti. I wrapped my arms around him tight and ran kisses all over his face.

Thank you baby, I love you soooo much, I said to him.

I love you to girl, now go on before y'all be late, he said handing me boss, and come to the house when you leave school.

OK, I said while buckling boss in his car seat, and climbing in starting my car.

The whole day was good, Dell even brought me lunch today, we talked, and he asked if we could be cool. Don't know what that's about, it sounded like bullshit, but maybe its not.

After school, me Kayla, MyMy, and Lola went over Langston's to practice a dance for tryouts, auntie was going to pick up boss because she had to take him to the doctor today.

Your kick needs to be stronger, Kayla told me.

But I can't kick with this leg for some reason, I said trying to kick my left leg, just as high as I kick with my right.

The front door opened and Langston walked in with his Lil brother gutta, and his bestfriend juju.

Hey baby, I said breathing heavy, and hugging him.

Was up, he said gripping my ass.

Was up y'all, he spoke to everybody else.

Hey, they all said

Was up sus, gutta said putting his arm around my shoulder once hustla let me go.

Was up, I said to him.

C'mere let me holla at chu, he said pulling me towards the back.

Don't be closing no doors in the room with that nigga, and them Lil bity ass shorts on, Langston yelled from the living room.

Shut up, I yelled back at him closing the door anyway.

Was up, I asked gutta.

Man who is that, he said nodding towards the living room.

I scrunched up my face, who, I asked putting my hands on my hips.

The one with the pink on, he said smiling.

I looked at him like he was crazy, un um, hell naw, nope, no, nooooo.

He laughed, cum on girl why you acting like that.

Cuz you're a ho gutta, and you're not finna play my girl, I said serious as hell.

Girl ain't nobody tryna play her, just tell her I said was up, he said still laughing.

Nope you're on your own with this one, I said brushing past him, and walking out the door.

When we got back in the living room, they had blunts in rotation, and hustla, and juju were burning on each other, They had us dying laughing. Once they caught the munchies they talked us into going to the store, and cooking. Kayla talked somebody at the liquor store into getting a bottle for us since we weren't old enough, and she got me a cake. After we ate, drunk, and sang happy birthday, everybody went home, I climbed in my bed and went straight to sleep

CHAPTER EIEGHTEEN

Yotti:

It felt good having a car, I couldn't sit my ass in the house for shit, as long as I was home before curfew, and answered whenever auntie called. Boss and I were picking out flowers, to visit Mell, and daddy's grave site. When I got there I cut my phone on airplane mode, I didn't wanna be bothered. I sat in between their tombstones, since they were married they were allowed to be side by side. I placed their roses on there grave, as tears begin to roll down my cheek.

I miss you so much daddy, I think about you every single day. I met a friend of yours, and I don't know how you would of felt about us if you were still here, but I really like him daddy, I said with a smile. I know you've never liked Dell, and even though I acted as if I didn't care if you liked him or not, your opinion mattered the most. I just thought that you didn't know Dell like I knew him, but you were right daddy he wasn't shit. I was skeptical about dating again, but its something about Langston, he makes me feel safe, and protected. No one could ever take your place, but when I'm with Langston he fills that space that left when you left.

I sat there in deep thought, I looked down at boss who had fallen asleep in my lap.

I was getting sleepy to so I got up and left, it was nowhere near my curfew, so I decided to go to Langston's. When I got there he was no where to be found, I laid boss in his bed, stripped down to my bra and panties, put on one if his T-shirts, and fell out.

Hustla:

I been blowing baby girl up all day, and she ain't answered or responded to my text. I don't know what's going on with me, but I been tripping lately. All I could think about was her, I've been wanting her for so long, and now that I finally got her I can't let her go. I zoomed through traffic tryna make this last drop, so I can go home.

I done came a long way, thanks to Money. When my daddy got locked up, and Money got knocked off, it left every thing to me, it feel so good to have niggas willing to do my dirt for me. I hated to get my hands dirty, because I didn't wanna end up like pops or Money, but don't get the shit twisted I'm a boss, so I gotta set some examples every now and then, I just prefer less drama. I dialed Yotti number again, and still nothing. I rode by her auntie house but didn't see her car, where the fuck they at, I spoke out loud, I ain't gone lie I miss both of them.

What it do, I answered the phone for my Lil brother.

Where ya at.

Finna pull up at the house.

Aight meet you there, he said then hung up

My Lil brother wanted to be like me so bad, but I wanted better for him. I didn't even want this shit for myself but my pops drug me in this shit. But it is what it is, I'm built for this my brother not, he to hot headed, and trigga happy. Without me he won't make it far, he acts before he thinks, but that's my Lil brother so I got him I make sure he keep his head straight.

I pulled up in my apartment complex, and seen Yotti car. I couldn't help the smile that appeared across my face.

Hustla, I heard somebody call me.

I turned around, damn, I thought, she was thick as fuck, she looked familiar but I couldn't put a name on it.

Who you is, I asked ion trust people, everybody looking for a come up.

Chanel, we have English together, she said smiling, showing her dimple.

Right, I remember you now, I said.

Oh, um it was nice seeing you, she said.

I knew that wasn't all she wanted to say, but she didn't have enough confidence yet.

You to, I said licking my lips, and smiling.

She turned and walked off, damn she was right. I had my mind made up I wanted to fuck Chanel, Yotti got a nigga on hold to.

I walked in the house and it was quite, I slipped my shoes off by the door, and walked towards the back. I peeped in boss room he was laid out, I walked to the master bedroom, and my baby was laying there sleep. I walked to the bed, took my pants off and climbed in beside her. I pulled her close to me, her Paris spry hitting my nose. I sat there and watched her sleep, when her phone started to vibrate. I don't know why but I picked it up and looked at it, I ain't never looked at a females phone, but Yotti is my baby, I care about what she doing when she ain't with me.

Text reads: I miss you so much girl, and I can't take being away from you no more, what happened to us I was yo world, and you gone let the next nigga take my spot. I would of never done no shit like that to you, you always came first and you know that. I know I fucked up and I'm truly sorry, but I gotta get chu back ASAP I'm missing you too much.

I knew it wasn't nobody but Dee bitch ass, everything in me wanted to wake her ass up and go off on her. But for what his bitch ass bothering her. The sound of the front door closing snapped me out of it, I deleted the message, and walked up front to holla at my brother.

CHAPTER NINETEEN

Yotti:

I woke up to voices in the front, I rubbed my eyes, I wanted to get up, but I couldn't move. I picked my phone up to see what time it was, it was going on 10:30. I scrolled thru my unread text and stopped at Lola's name.

Text reads: I got something to tell u call me asap.

So, I called her.

Girl everybody been looking for you all day, where you been at, she said picking up the phone.

Um hello to you to, I've been sleep, I went to visit daddy, then I came to Langston's and went to sleep, but was up, I asked her.

Well first off, Dee is going around asking for yo new number,

You didn't give it to him did you, I asked cutting her off, shid we may be on speaking terms, but he don't need to be calling me.

Naw, but I did ask him what he want, he said he miss you, and want y'all to work it out, she said.

I sighed, next, Dell can miss me with that shit.

OK and guess who's tryna talk to me, she said.

Who, I semi yelled she bet not say

Gutta, she said before I finished my thought.

I got quite, I really didn't know what to say, I mean gutta a cool person but I know how he handles females. I ain't the one to throw salt, but at the same time that's my girl and I gotta give her the heads up.

He's cool, but dealing with a person like him you have to be able to accept what comes with that lifestyle, I told her.

What you mean Yotti he's no different from hustla, she said sounding offended.

Trust me the same thing I just told you I told myself, I'm not tryna stop you from fucking with him I'm just saying don't let your guard down to soon, I told her.

I feel you, but you know I don't tolerate bullshit, I'll get some act right in his ass, she said as we laughed.

We wrapped up our convo, and I got up to go in the living room, hustla, and gutta were playing the game while boss was pulling out shit.

Was up baby, hustla said without taking his eyes off the t.v.

Hey, I said before turning to go in the kitchen, I was hungry, they had ordered pizza so I got a couple of slices.

I bit into my pizza, then I felt hands wrap around my waist.

I missed you where you been at, Langston asked me.

I went to see daddy today, then came here and went to sleep, I said while turning to face him.

I want y'all to spend the night with me, he said while rubbing my stomach.

You know auntie ain't going for that, I said being realistic.

I'll call her, he said before walking back to the living room.

I followed behind him, and sat on the couch beside boss.

After ending his conversation with auntie, he hung up laughing.

What's funny, I asked.

She said cool, you better be at school tomorrow, and you better come home from school still a virgin, he said as he and gutta laughed.

I rolled my eyes, and picked boss up so he could take a bath.

After bathing him, and finally getting him to sleep, I went to Langston's room to shower. When I got out all the lights were off except for our room and our bathroom, Langston was laying across the bed smoking. I walked to the dresser to get some lotion, I sat on the edge of the bed and begin to put it on as he watched my every move. I grabbed my bra and panties from my dresser, and a big T-shirt from his. He climbed out the bed going into the bathroom, cutting the shower on. I layed in bed, and waited till he got out. He got out, put boxers on, and climbed in pulling me close to him.

I wrapped my arms around his neck, as his hands fell on my waist, and ass.

I missed you today too, I said.

He leaned forward and kissed my lips, slipping his tongue in my mouth.

I want you girl, can I have you, he asked while planting soft kiss on my neck.

I 'm your's Langston, you know I can care less about another nigga, I said with a smile.

Naw I mean this, he said while pulling my panties to the side running his hand across my pearl.

I moved his hand, im not ready Langston.

He sighed, then climbed out the bed going to the bathroom, I knew something was wrong because he closed the door, he never close the door if its just us.

I don't know what to do, I just wasn't ready, I've already made him wait months, and its not like he will play me like hit, and leave. He's invested to much money in me so I know we're together, I just was scared. The bathroom door opened, and he was fully clothed.

Where are you going, I asked.

I need to clear my head, he said walking out the room.

I got up and followed him, if you need space Langston we'll leave.

I didn't say that, he sighed, I just don't know what you want me to do, I've done everything I could to show you I'm for you and only you, I don't live with bitches, but I got this place for you, everything you need you get, I see you naked all the time what you scared of, he asked.

He was right, this is my man, and if he's not being satisfied at home he'll find satisfaction elsewhere. I didn't say anything I just grabbed his hand and led him to the room. I kissed his lips as I unbuttoned his pants, he stepped out of his shoes, and pants, and pulled his shirt off. He laid me on the bed, pulling my shirt off, he laid on top of me kissing me gently. He pulled my bra off and ran his tongue across my nipples, as his free hand slid my panties off.

hustla

She smelled so good, her body was so soft. I pulled her panties off, and begin to play with her juice box. I could feel her heart pounding, so I took my time with her. I lifted her legs, spreading them apart, I sniffed her box, she smelled good as fuck. I ran my tongue across her pearl, licking fast, then slow, then sucking it gently, as she arched her back. I lifted her hips licking her juice box till her legs begin to shake. I lifted up, she had a smile on her face. I rubbed my head against her perl, then moved it down to her opening but she stopped me.

Do you have a condom, she asked me.

Damn you don't trust me, I said laughing, and reaching in my nightstand.

I put it on and pressed against her whole, she jumped.

You love me, I asked her.

Yes, she said.

Just relax, I got chu, I told her while pushing myself inside her.

She gripped my back tight, while digging her nails in, but she felt too good, she was warm, wet, and tight as hell, S/o to Money for keeping her pure for me.

The next morning I woke up happy as hell, my baby was sleep wit a smile on her face. She looked peaceful so I let her sleep while I got boss ready for daycare. After everybody got dressed, they followed me to Hardee's to get some breakfast, then went to school.

When I got in my English class Chanel walked in and sat right beside me.

Hey, she spoke.

Was up, I said to her.

I licked my lips, she looked good as fuck today, she blushed when she noticed me looking at her.

Was that your girlfriend, she asked out the blue.

Huh, who, I asked laughing

With the white car like yours, she said.

Yea, that's my girl, I said, shit I felt like the conversation was over after that.

But we can be friends tho, you should give me your number, she said serious as hell, I just told her I got a gal.

I laughed, I just told you I got a gal, why you want my number.

You don't have to have relations with every girl you meet, its OK to make some your friends, she said laughing.

What's yours, I said pulling out my minute phone.

She looked at me then grabbed it to put her number in.

Yotti:

Spill it ya bish, MyMy said laughing as we stood at our locker's.

What? I asked her.

You been smiling since you walked in here, you ain't that damn happy about School, its too early for that shit, she said serious faced.

I couldn't help but to laugh, I was about to spill it when Dell walked up.

Yo can I holla at you for a min, he said.

I looked at MyMy, she rolled her eyes and walked off. She didn't care for Dell, she liked me and Langston together tho.

Was up, I said leaning against my locker.

Did you get my text, he asked.

What text, you don't even have my number, I said getting aggravated already.

I miss you Yotti, I can't do this no more, do you know how it feel seeing you with that nigga, you mine and you know that, he said

Was yours, if you wanted to be with me that bad you would of did right from jump, the only reason you're even in my face now is cuz I'm with him, get the fuck outta here with that shit, and you got a babymama, I said as I brushed past him he has officially ruined my day.

CHAPTER TWENTY

Three months later.

Hustla:

I was out getting fitted for my tux for prom. I wasn't even gone go but Yotti talked me into it. I think she just really want me to show her off to the girls at my school, but I was cool with that she got them hoes beat hands down. My phone started vibrating in my pocket, it was Chanel. Chanel tried to play that role like she didn't wanna fuck wit me cuz of my girl, but Chanel quickly hops on this dick whenever I tell her to. We got a understanding, she know I got a gal, so she stay in her lane, but she don't take no shit either, the minute I slow down on showing her attention she gets in my shit. Chanel is older then Yotti, she got more experience, I guess that's why I can't stop fucking with her.

Was up girl, I said answering the phone for her.

Hey what you doing, she asked.

Finna leave this tux place what's up, I said while paying for my tux.

I wanna see you, she said.

Let me see what I can do, I told her shid I had to find out where my girl was first.

She sighed, there you go with that shit.

With what you know I got a gal Cha, don't start that shit man, let me see where she at first, I said.

Whatever, she said hanging up in my face

I laughed as I hoped on the interstate, heading to the trap, she'll be aight, she ain't going nowhere she stuck on me.

A couple hours later I was on my way home, I pulled over to get some gas and ran into Alicia.

Long time no see, she said walking towards me.

Was up licia, what you been up to, I asked her as I pumped my gas.

The last time I talked to her she threatened to beat me and Yotti's ass, but that was months ago.

Same ol same ol, you still with that bitch, she said.

What I tell you about calling her a bitch, I said.

My bad homewrecker then, she said putting her hands on her hips.

The home was already wreaked before she came, I said putting the cap on my gas pump.

I turned to get in my car when she stopped me.

How, what did I do to make you go out and cheat on me, she semi yelled.

I didn't cheat on you, and you didn't do shit but sit around and spend up my money, if I would of had a set back I couldn't depend on you to help me bounce back, I said to her.

I hoped in my car and pulled off, she was old news. When I pulled up at the house, I didn't see baby car, so I walked two buildings over to Chanel's.

Hey, she said as she opened the door, with some Lil bity shorts on.

Was up, I said walking straight to her room.

I laid across her bed, as she straddled my lap. She reached over on her dresser and pulled out a rolled up blunt, she fired it up while taking the remote control turning the radio on.

We smoked till she got horny, I just laid back and let her do her, or let her do me. I was so high and weak when we got finished, I dozed off. I kept feeling my phone buzz on my face, my eyes shot open. I looked down at Chanel who was curled up under me knocked out, I slipped from beside her and begin to put my shit on. I walked outside and was hit by darkness, damn how long was I sleep, I looked at my phone as I begin walking back to the house, I had 10 missed calls on each phone from her, and text messages. The more I begin to read the funkier she was talking I know she pissed. I walked in the house, and I could hear her on the phone going off on somebody, she was so mad she was talking Spanish. I walked in the kitchen cuz I smelled food but it was clean as hell in there. Fuck the food at, I thought as I popped the microwave open. I licked my lips as I cut the microwave on to heat up my food.

Fuck you been at, she asked coming from outta nowhere.

Handling something for my Lil brother, I lied.

That's funny since your brother stopped by here with Lola today, and no you, she said.

Baby please don't start today, feel like I been hearing bitches nag all day.

She laughed and walked to the back, I sat there eating my food, and playing the game when I heard the front door slam.

Baby, I hollered out but she didn't answer,

I sat my plate down, and jumped up running to the door by the time I got on the porch the only thing I could see was her tail lights.

Yotti:

Hustla got me fucked up if he think he gonna start that lying shit. My day started off perfect, until my encounter with Dell, it went down hill from there, this bitch that I got 3rd block with name Kionna approached me asking do I mess with hustla. I'm like wtf he doesn't even go to this school so who is this bitch asking about my dude.

Flashback

Naw I don't mess with him that's my dude Kionna you know that, I said confused as fuck.

Naw that's my cousin Alicia boyfriend, she told me about you tryna get with him, I thought you were with Dell she said.

I laughed, look girl today ain't the day , Alicia knows who he belong too, and why the fuck do you care its none of your business, like who the fuck is she to be checking me over a nigga she ain't even fucked.

I'm jus saying when she mentioned your name, I was like she cool we got class together, then she started telling me how messy you were, she said.

Bitch we ain't even cool like that, why the fuck am I even still talking to you, I said walking off.

When school ended I walked outside to the word bitch keyed on my car I've been pissed every since.

Flashback over

I walked in the house to boss hollering and screaming. I walked in his room and he was standing in the corner, as Kayla sat in the rocking chair making sure he didn't move.

Ya Ya, he said wen he saw me, he tried to run to me but Kayla stopped him.

Aaaaaaat get back over there I don't care cause she here, she said to him.

What he do, I asked her.

He broke my fucking Nicki perfume, she said frustrated.

I turned and walked out the room I hated to see my baby in trouble. I kicked my shoes off, and flopped on my bed, I looked down at my ringing phone, Langston, I hit the ignore button I didn't wanna talk to his lying ass right now, I probably want say shit to him till prom.

The more I sat there the more I started to think, he and Alicia ain't been together in almost a year, so why would kionna just now say something about me and him. And today when I went to his house his car was home, but he wasn't. Hustla always drives his car, so where was he. I hated to think he was cheating on me but these last couple of weeks he's been acting funny. Every since the first time we did it all I could think about was him it would crush me if I find out he's cheating on me. I love Langston, and I can't see myself away from him no time soon. My thoughts were interrupted by a knock at the back door.

I opened the door once I saw it was hustla, I turned to walk back to my room as he shut and locked the door.

What's yo problem, he asked sitting on the bed beside me.

Are you still fucking Alicia, I asked getting straight to the point.

What? Hell naw where the fuck you get that dumb ass shit from, he said.

I told him the story.

Somebody keyed your car, he asked.

I nodded my head yea,

Don't worry about it, just drive my car tomorrow, and I'll take care of yours when I leave school, he said like it was nothing.

Where were you today, I asked him.

I told you girl, I went to get a tux, then went to handle something for my brother, he said.

I just left it alone. We cuddled and watched movies the rest of the night, I got my mind made up, fuck what the next bitch talm bout I know where my man belong, and im not letting him go no time soon.

CHAPTER TWENTY- ONE

Yotti:

Day of prom

Lola, and I were at the hair salon getting our hair done for prom. Gutta asked Lola to go, I was actually happy, I'll have somebody I know with me. In two hours, we had to meet Kayla and MyMy at the nail shop. After finishing everything I went home to get dressed. Aunt Chell was doing my make up when somebody knocked on the door, Kayla went to open it, I figured it wasn't nobody but Langston.

Hold still Yotti, my auntie said as she tried to put my eye shadow on.

You mind if I do your lashes a familiar voice said, but I haven't heard that voice in years.

Nyla, I said as I turned to be face to face with my mother.

She smiled slightly, what the fuck was she doing here I haven't seen her in almost 3 years, she hasn't called to check on me or nothing. My eyes begin to water, as so much shit ran thru my mind. I'm not gone cry today, its Langston's senior prom, I'm not going to fuck up his day being a cry baby.

Sure, you can do my lashes, I said.

Auntie moved out the way, is this your daughter Nyla, I heard her say.

I spun around and noticed the Lil girl standing there for the first time, the Lil girl smiled at me. I have a sister that looks exactly like me, and how sad is it that she's damn near two and I'm just now meeting her. Let it go Yotti, that's the past you're happy now, rather she came then or now your mother came, I told myself.

Hi, I said to her.

She just smiled showing the three top teeth she had.

We'll be downstairs, my auntie said taking my sister with her, they closed the door once everybody left.

She started my lashes, it was a big awkward silence, it was so much I wanted to say, but I didn't wanna get angry. I looked down at her leg, thank god she had on pants, cuz I didn't wanna be reminded of that day.

Here you go, she said handing me the mirror, so I could see my face.

She did a damn good job, thanks, I said as I stood up.

You look beautiful, she commented.

Thanks, I said as I put my shoes on.

You mind if I take a picture of you, she asked.

I looked at her, after tryna avoid eye contact, sure, I posed as she snapped several pictures.

Yotti I'm sorry, she started to say.

Not today Nyla please I don't wanna ruin my makeup, I said.

OK I can agree, but it's a lot I want to get off my chest, she said.

Maybe we can do lunch one day, I suggested as I looked myself over in the mirror.

I would like that, she said.

We exchanged numbers, and headed downstairs with everyone else.

What's her name, I asked her as we walked down the steps.

Yasmin, she said with a smile.

She looks like daddy, I said it was the truth tho.

He does have strong Gene's, she said.

I stopped in my tracks, are you saying that's my daddy's child, when I said she looked like daddy I didn't actually think she was his, hell I didn't even know daddy was still creeping with her.

Yes, she is, she said.

We turned the corner, and my eyes fell on Langston, he looked so sexy in a suit.

Hustla's your date, Nyla said as we got closer to them.

No that's my man, I said as I wrapped my arms around him.

You look good girl, he said smiling from ear to ear.

Thanks, you do to, I said as we posed for the many flashes that went off.

After taking a ton of pictures, we were finally pulling up at prom. Lola, and gutta looked good together, and they looked happy. It felt like Every female we passed spoke to hustla, and gutta, but starred at me and Lola with the stank face. I don't know about Lola but it was making my day. Daddy always said if you ain't got haters, you ain't doing something right, so I must be doing a damn good job.

I lined up with Langston, to do his senior walk.

You look good bae, I said as I begin to fix his tie.

He pulled me closer, you know I can't wait to take this dress off you, he said in my ear, I just giggled, and blushed.

Chanel (cha):

You know I can't wait to take this dress off you, I heard him whisper to her.

It made my skin crawl, I hated the fact that both our last names started with the same letter, because of reasons like this, I have to stand behind him and his bitch for senior walk at prom. His girlfriend was actually pretty, but I couldn't stand to see them together. I should of stayed away when he told me he had a girl, but I've been liking him since junior year. My plan was to take him from her, but he was actually in love with her, now I'm stuck on him. Sometimes I feel so stupid, he made it clear from jump about her, but I just had to go there now

I can't stop thinking about him, I can't stop looking at him, or her.

You aight, my date asked me.

I smiled and nodded my head.

The faculty called his and her name, as they walked across stage. I handed them the paper with me and my dates name on it, they called our name as we walked across.

I saw them sit at a table with gutta and some girl, I've never seen before. I smiled when I saw my girl coco sitting at the table beside them, I flew over there, and sat in the seat closest to hustla, I could hear everything they were talking about.

Come dance with me Lola, I could hear his girlfriend say as Beyonce 7/11 came on. They got up to dance and they actually looked cute doing the routine they were doing; they drew attention from girls from the majorette squad. I rolled my eyes cuz the hoes on our majorette squad swear they had to battle everywhere they went.

I watched as the started to battle in there on section, but everybody was surrounding them tryna watch, I got up and walked over there, and they showed out on our majorettes, I'm not a hater by far they did that.

Hustla:

My baby looked good as fuck out there dancing. The majorettes walked up and asked Lola and Yotti if they wanted to battle, they laughed at they ass but battled anyway, Yotti wasn't turning down no challenge. They killed it; they had the whole crowd rocking with them. I looked over and saw Chanel starring at Yotti, hell she been starring at us all night as long as she didn't open her mouth, I didn't give a fuck tho. She turned and walked to the punch bowl when she noticed me starring at her, I don't know why but I followed her.

You look good, I said walking up behind her, I reached around her to get a cup.

Thanks, you do to, she said, but I could tell something was wrong with her.

I felt small hands grip the back of my tux, could you get me some too, Yotti asked as she stood in the middle of me and Chanel.

I handed her my cup and begin to fix me another drink. She downed it and excused herself as she walked around Chanel to throw it away.

Let's dance, she said as she kissed my lips.

I noticed Chanel roll her eyes as I thru my empty cup away. I pulled Yotti in front of me resting my hands on her hips as she led me to the dance floor to dance to Tamar Braxton's all the way home. She wrapped her arms around my neck, as I put one hand on her lower back, and the other on her ass. She looked and smelled so good I wanted to bend her over and fuck her right then and there. Everybody got seated as they got ready to announce the king and queen.

It's now the moment everyone has been waiting for, we've had a close call, but we finally have the king and queen, Mrs. Murphy announced.

I wanna say congratulations to all who were nominated, but let's give it up for our king Langston Harris, she said

I just sat there who the fuck put me up for nominations I don't do shit like this.

Go up there, Yotti said as she pinched my hand.

I sighed, as I got up, and walked up there, they crowned me.

And to our queen Chanel Hughes, Mrs. Murphy said.

She walked up there with a smile on her face, as they crowned her.

Now everyone clears the floor so the king and queen can give us a dance, Mrs. Murphy said as Beyonce dance for you came on.

This got to be a fucking joke, not only did they pick the longest song, but they also picked the song that Chanel and I fucked to several times. I grabbed her hand and led her off stage to the dance floor. She wrapped her hands around my neck as I placed mine on her back.

I glanced at Yotti who was sitting there watching. It's crazy there playing our song huh, Chanel said in my ear.

Yeah, it is, I said.

I can't keep my mind off you, she said as she pulled herself closer to me, so close that if we looked each other in the face we'd be kissing.

Please don't do that shit here Cha, I told her.

I can't help it you're all I think about, she said.

I just stopped dancing and walked off.

Yotti:

I sat there watching Langston dance with the queen, it didn't bother me at first, till she scooted closer to him saying something. Whatever she said must of pissed him off, cause he walked of the dance floor.

Let's go, he said walking up to me.

After we left we went out to eat, and back to his place.

The minute we walked through the door he was all over me sucking, and kissing all over my neck.

Baby wait, let me get out of my dress first, I said while laughing.

He helped me out of my dress, he lifted me up and carried me to the bed. I sat there in my bra and panties, and watched him strip down to his boxers. He climbed on top of me kissing my lips, as he unsnapped my bra, then pulled my panties off. He went down to eat me, as I felt my legs begin to shake. This was our Fourth time doing it and I swear it got better every time. He flicked his tongue across my pearl which caused me to moan. He came up licking his glistening lips, you taste good, he said with a smile.

He opened my legs as wide as they would go, and rubbed his thick throbbing dick against my pearl.

Do you have a condom, I asked it wasn't that I didn't trust him I just didn't wanna get pregnant I got goals to accomplish.

Naw, he said as he slid inside of me.

He bit down on his bottom lip as he begin to thrust in and out of me.

Take it out Langston, I barely got out, I ain't gone lie it felt so much better without the condom, he was so warm and hard.

It's in there now he said as he held my legs up going as deep as he could.

He pulled out, I looked down as prenut oozed out of his head, get on top, he said as he laid on the bed.

I climbed on top of him, he grabbed my waist, and he begin to guide me. I leaned forward causing my Breast to bounce in his face.

Damn girl, he said as he cupped my Breast licking each nipple causing them to grow hard.

He held on to my back as I finally got the hang of ridding, he ran his tongue up my neck, to my chin, to my lips kissing me passionately.

You feel so good girl, he moaned.

It felt so good I couldn't say shit but moan. He lifted both my legs holding me up by my thighs, as he begin to lift me up and down on his dick my legs begin to shake, as I felt my nut coming.

Damn girl what she doing down there, he said as he felt my pussy muscles tighten around his dick.

He gripped my thighs tighter, as I exploded all over his dick, fuck , he grunted as he begin to throb hard inside of me. Shit, he said out of breath as he eased his limp stick out of me. I was so weak I couldn't move, he got up and cleaned himself off, then washed me off. He climbed in bed beside me wrapping his arms around me tight.

I love you tise, he said planting kisses on my neck.

I love you to Langston.

CHAPTER TWENTY-TWO

Chanel:

2 months later

I sat in the car after leaving the doctors office. After missing my period twice in a row, I immediately made a doctors appointment. I just thank god that I was able to graduate before getting pregnant, I didn't know how to tell hustla. I know the first thing he gone say is get an abortion, but I wasn't about to kill my baby, I guess it's between me and you, I said out loud talking to the baby.

Hustla:

I nodded my head to Lil boosie betrayed, as I rode around my city, I was going to meet up with Kai. I know what y'all thinking ain't that Dee friend, it is but we doing business together, and I ain't turning down no money, Even if he got a pussy as a friend.

Watup my nigga, I dapped him off as he hoped in my car.

Watup, watup, he said back.

I reached in the back pulling out a Louis duffle bag, and gave it to him. He dug in his pocket pulling out a knot, I popped the rubber band and begin counting my money as he checked the product.

You straight, he asked once he was satisfied with the shit in the bag.

Yea, we good, I said once I counted all the money.

Aight, ima hit you up next week, he said getting out the car.

Do DAT, I said as he closed the door and I pulled off.

I don't know what him and Dee got going on but he been buying work from me for bout a month and a half now. Yotti said they fell out but shid that ain't my business, I'm just tryna do business and stack this paper. Now that I'm out of school I been going hard in these streets, niggas know I got it, so my income has tripled. Yotti hated that shit to but I gotta get this money, I done fucked around and got her pregnant the night of prom. Her auntie was PISSED she went off on us, but I swore on my life that my son, my gal, and my seed gone be straight regardless. She cried, about how she wasn't gone finish school, but ima make sure she get that diploma even if it kills me. Chell let them come live with me, she said they my responsibility now. That's why I'm in these streets so hard, Yotti say I'm never home but I gotta get dis money I got four mouths to feed.

Baby, I called out when I walked in the house.

Ssshhhhh, boss sleep, she said sticking her head out the kitchen.

I walked in and wrapped my arms around her waist, as she seasoned some pork chops.

Juju came by here looking for you, she said.

What he want, I asked her.

He left a black bag in the closet, she said.

Where my kiss at girl, she laughed then turned to peck my lips.

You missed daddy, I said

I always miss daddy, she said blushing.

You betta, I said as I walked out the kitchen to my room.

I walked in the closet and shuffled through all her shit, till I found the bag, I shut the closet door, sat on the floor and opened the bag.

My nigga, my nigga, I said rubbing my hands together.

I pulled out the money machine and begin to count the money. I smiled once it counted the last stack displaying 100 thousand. I put the money back, and hid my machine, I looked down at my buzzing phone Chanel, not today I thought.

I walked out the closet to Yotti walking into the room.

C'mere let me show you something, I said pulling her to the dresser.

What, she asked.

This, I said putting her hand on my brick in my pants.

She smiled as she stuck her hands in my pants wrapping her soft hands around my dick.

You know I hate quickies, she said massaging my shift.

Just get daddy right, I got you when I get home, I said as I sat her on top of the dresser.

I opened her robe, and played with her till she got wet, I pulled her to the edge, and slid in, damn she got some good pussy I thought.

After we cleaned up, she went back to the kitchen, and I was finna get back to this money.

Dinner should be ready by seven,

Aight, I said as I kissed her lips, and left out the door.

As I was walking to get in the car I saw Chanel car turning in. I need to move asap, I hate that her and my girl live in the same apartment complex.

Her car slowed down when she saw me, keep going, I thought. I hoped in the car as she rolled by, i pulled off.

I hoped on the interstate, my phone started buzzing, Chanel, this time I answered.

Yea,

I need to talk to you, she said.

Was up, I asked.

In person, she said sounding frustrated.

I'm busy cha, what is it, I said getting aggravated.

Well get unbusy before I walk down there and tell your girl what's going on, she snapped before hanging up.

Maaaannnnn, I said frustrated females show will stress a nigga out, I texted her the address to my spot, she gotta be a fool to think I'm coming to her house and my gal up the street. I ain't gone sit up here and say Cha don't mean nothing to me I fucks with her, and she knows that but she know where my home is.

I pulled up at the spot, and waited till I seen her car pull up. I got out and hoped in her car, I looked over at her gas hand it was on E, it was a habit to look at her and Yotti gas hand whenever I got in their car.

Go to the gas station girl, the minute you break down you gone be calling me to come get you, I told you quit riden like that, I snapped at her.

She pulled off driving to the nearest gas station.

Why you look like that, I asked her.

Why did she look like that I asked myself, she had the same glow as yotti.

Like what, she asked as she pulled into the gas station.

I pulled out a 100 and gave it to her, here fill it up, and bring me back some Swisher sweets, I told her.

She climbed out to go pay, damn her ass has gotten bigger I thought.

I looked down and saw a folded up piece of paper with her name on it, that looked like a doctors note. They say when you look for shit you find it, I picked that paper up and wanted to shit a brick wen I saw positive on it. I seen her coming out of the store, I put the paper down and got out to pump the gas. I just starred at her, as she climbed in the car.

Let me guess you went thru my stuff, she asked as soon as I sat my ass in the seat.

Is that what you had to tell me, I asked her.

She didn't say nothing.

Cha quit fucking playn and let me know what's up, I snapped

Yes that's what I had to tell you now what, she snapped back.

I picked the paper up to check the date, she just got it. 16 weeks mannnn Yotti gone kill me, its too late for an abortion.

Now what, she asked again.

Have you ate, I asked her.

Earlier, she said.

Let's go to chilli's,

Yotti:

I sat Langston's plate in the microwave, I knew he'll be walking thru the door any minute now he was never late for dinner.

So, what do you think about Lexington, if it's a girl, I asked Nyla

Our relationship has gotten better over these last couple of months. We talked about a lot of our differences, and she explained of why she was acting the way she was.

Lexington is pretty, Lexington Yatise Harris, she said

I like that, I said

I heard keys at the door, I looked at my phone it was 6:45, I smiled.

Was up y'all, he said as he bent down to kiss me.

Hey, I said.

Where the kids at, he asked as he sat down and begin to roll a blunt.

They're gone can you go in there with that shit, I said scrunching up my face.

Damn I'm not gone smoke around yo fat ass, I can't sit down and roll my blunt, he snapped.

What the fuck is his problem I thought, naw but you can take yo damn shoes off walking around on my carpet, with yo dirty ass feet, I snapped back.

I looked at his shoes and it didn't have a spot of dirt on it, but he snapped on me so I had to snap back.

Mann, he said as he passed Nyla the weed he had broke down, and a rello and got up and left.

Hustla

My mind was fucked up, I just wanted to get high and clear my mind, and she with that bullshit.

Where the fuck you going, she semi yelled as she yanked the back of my shirt.

I don't know why but I snapped, quit fucking grabbing on my shirt, I said as I pushed her.

She stumbled, but caught her balance, her whole face dropped, as she rushed me her hands was swinging fast as fuck. I grabbed her and slammed her on the hood of my car, and tried to hold her down but she kept swinging and kicking.

Get the fuck off me, she growled, as she grabbed my shirt stretching it.

Man let my shirt go, I said she was pissing me off.

What are yall doing, I heard Nyla say.

I pulled her hands off me, and backed up I bent down to pick up my keys, she ran and pushed me causing me to fall.

Yotti stop, Nyla said as she grabbed her.

I jumped up I wanted to hit her ass so bad, I reached around Nyla, and grabbed Yotti hair.

I swear if I didn't love yo ass I woulda busted yo shit wide open, I said as I pulled her face close to mine, then pushed her back.

Nyla held her back as I walked and got in my car.

Don't bring yo dirty ass to my house either, she yelled as I pulled off.

What the fuck type of shit she on, I just wanted to come home smoke and lay next to her but fuck her.

I met up with juju later that night at the strip club, but that didn't do shit but get a nigga on brick, and I can't even go home.

Wyd? Cha, I said to Chanel as I sat in the parking lot of Lucky's.

Its 2 in the morning what you think I'm doing, she said in a groggy tone.

Can I come over, I asked her.

She sighed, I'm finna unlock the door, she said before hanging up.

I pulled off in that direction, I really wanted to be next to my baby tho, I've never missed a night since we moved together. I picked up my phone and called her, she hit ignore on my ass.

I stripped down to my boxers, and climbed next to Cha. I wrapped my arms around her, pulling her close to me, she smelled good but I wanted to smell Yotti.

Babymama must of put that ass out, she said.

She trippen right now, I said

I grabbed her hand and put it on my stick, she smiled, she know what time it is.

CHAPTER TWENTY-THREE

Yotti:

I rolled over Saturday morning, and Langston really didn't bring his ass home last night. I was beyond pissed; he's never missed a night since we moved in together. I jumped up and ran to the bathroom, I felt nauseated, ugh I can't wait till this shit is over with. After brushing my teeth, and washing my face, I started to straighten up the house when Kayla called.

Hello, I answered.

Put sum clothes on were on our way to get you, she said.

Aight, I said as we hung up.

I showered and put clothes on, they pulled up a hr later.

Can we go to cracker barrel, I'm hungry ass hell, I said as soon as I climbed in.

When we got there everybody had some shit going on in there life and needed to vent especially me so I went first.

Me and hustla got into it yesterday, I said as I looked over my menu.

Why, MyMy asked scrunching up her face.

I really can't even tell you, he came home with a attitude, and snapped on me cause I told him not to smoke in my living room, I said thinking about the whole incident.

Hi I'm David, your server , can I get you ladies something to drink.

We placed our drink orders, and continued talking.

But I've seen hustla smoke plenty of times in your living room, what was different last night, Lola asked.

Cause I was in there he know I don't like when he smoke around me, I said as the server brought our drinks, and took our order.

So what he say when you told him that, MyMy asked.

He snapped on me, I told them the entire story word from word, and they gone say I was in the wrong.

Are y'all serious, I don't give a fuck who pissed him off, I didn't do shit to him so when you hit my doorstep leave the attitude outside, what the fuck, I said confused that they would even think that.

But still that's his house, you saw he had an attitude you should of just let him get high and calm his nerves, he wasn't doing nothing but rolling up, he said he wasn't gone smoke in front of you, you should of left it alone, Kayla said.

She was right I did just snap on him, the waiter sat our food down, I said my grace and dug in my shit like I ain't ate in days.

My turn, Lola said.

Well I really don't have issues, I just need some advice, she said.

Spill it, MyMy said.

So gutta and I have been spending a lot of time lately, and he asked me to be his girl, but I really don't do D-boys, but I like him alot, she said.

MyMy laughed, and why you don't do D-boys, shid they turn me on, she said as we all laughed.

Because its too much to deal with, you gotta worry about bitches, long nights, police, haters, and did I say bitches, Lola said as we laughed again.

You right it is a lot, hell hustla don't come in till 3 or 4 in the morning, and that shit gets on my nerves, I said.

Not all D-boys are like that, Kayla and Kai don't have problems, MyMy said

Bullshit, we have our problems like every body else we just know how to solve our differences, Kayla said.

So Kai's cheated on you before, I asked.

She shrugged, first of all Kai is sneaky, if and I said if he has or is cheating on me he will not let that shit get back to me, Kai don't play that shit he leaves the streets in the streets, he never mix his business or pleasure life with his personal life, if Kai cheats he's not gone fuck a bitch that talk to damn much, he to scared ima fuck him up, she said.

Hustla never cheated on me from what I know of, I said.

This my thing tho 90% of niggas cheat, just don't let me find out. If he can't put his hoes in their place I don't want him. Like if you got a gal at home, and you fuck off where a rubber, niggas be so stupid pretend to be faithful, but the minute wifey catch something, or find out he got somebody pregnant, the nigga wanna catch a attitude, you cheated, and didn't wrap it up, why you mad, Kayla said.

I'm just saying Kai and I have been together for six years, everything isn't gone be peaches and cream, you jus gotta determine if that person is worth going thru hell and back with, Kayla said.

That's why I love Kayla she keep it real and don't sugar coat shit, her and Kai ain't nothing but 19, but they love each other, and go hard for each other, no matter what she put him thru, and vise versa. I look up to their relationship, and want one like it.

My turn, a random approached me the other day talm bout she pregnant by Marco, MyMy said.

Well did you ask him, I asked.

Yea but he denied it, she said

Well ain't shit you can do about that but wait, Kayla said.

Marco is MyMy's boyfriend they've been together for like forever. Now that I think about it they were friends before she and I even met.

How long have you and Marco been messing around, I asked as I dug thru my purse to pay for my food.

I've known him all my life, but we got a Lil curious around 12, she said.

A Lil curious, you've been knowing him for 17 years, hell 18 next week, he popped that cherry at 12 bitch quit lyin, Kayla said, I was dying laughing.

Where to next, Kayla asked.

I looked down at my buzzing phone, it was hustla. I smiled hell I wasn't even mad at him no more I missed him last night.

Hello, I said.

Where you, he asked.

I'm out with Kayla nem, wasup, I asked him.

Tell her meet me somewhere I miss you, he said.

We ended up meeting him at a gas station, but we were closer so we got there first.

Let me out I gotta pee, I said.

Ugh they bathroom probably nasty, Kayla said.

So bitch I cant hold it I'll squat, you got some baby wipes in here, I asked

Here, she said passing me the wipes.

I'm going with you, MyMy said as we climbed out the car.

We walked out the store and bumped right into Alicia, and Kionna.

Excuse me, I said as I brushed past them.

I know excuse you bitch, Alicia said.

Who the fuck is you talking to I ain't said shit to you, I said.

You don't have to say shit I just don't like you, she said.

Whatever Alicia, I said laughing, and turning to walk off.

What's up then Yotti, she said balling her fist up.

Girl I'm pregnant I'm not gonna stand out here and fight you over old shit, I snapped.

Shid I will, MyMy said as she hauled off and smacked the shit outta Alicia.

Hustla

I pulled into the gas station, and damn near had a panic attack, when I saw my gal out there fighting with my baby. I thru my shit in park and hoped out, it was bout four fights, but my concern was Yotti. She was locked up on the ground with some girl.

Let my hair go bitch, Yotti said.

Naw bitch you let me go, the girl said back.

I wrapped my arms around Yotti waist and lifted her up, the girl let Yotti go, but Yotti still had the girl hair, she drug the girl right with us and was beating her all in the Head.

Let her go bae, I said,.

She let the girl go, the girl hoped up, and rushed us.

So you gone get this bitch pregnant, the girl yelled running towards us.

Alicia! I yelled when I finally realized who it was.

I put Yotti down and pulled her behind me, she tried to reach around me and swing at Yotti but I pushed her ass hard ass hell.

Hoe you tripping if you think you gone hit my babymama in front of me, I yelled when I pushed her.

Police, police, somebody from the crowd yelled out.

Everybody scattered like roaches, jumping in cars pulling off.

Follow me, I yelled to Kayla.

She nodded her head as we pulled off.

When we got back to the house I went off on all them.

What the fuck is wrong with y'all, what happened, I semi yelled as I rolled up a blunt to calm my nerves

No whats wrong with your bitches, pregnant or not I'm not taking nobody's shit, Yotti snapped back.

I sighed I really didn't wanna argue with her I missed her, I don't like when we beef.

C-mere baby let me holla at you, I said as I got up and walked to the room.

Don't do that shit baby, I hate arguing with you, I told her.

She wrapped her arms around my neck, and kissed me.

I love you Langston, she said.

I love you too girl, now get rid of yo girls so we can go get boss and go somewhere, I told her.

OK, she said smiling.

Get yo hair together first tho, I said as I started laughing.

CHAPTER TWENTY-FOUR

Kayla:

After dropping MyMy and Lola off, I decided to go to the mall to find something to wear for MyMy's surprise party Saturday. I ran my fingers thru my thick curls, and applied more lip stick before climbing out the car. I shopped around till finally finding an outfit, I turned to walk to the counter to ask for a dressing room. I tried the outfit on and looked myself over in the mirror. Once I approved I changed, and headed out the dressing room, bumping into Dee, what the fuck he doing in a women's store I thought.

Damn, was up Kayla, he said looking me up and down licking his lips.

I turnt my nose up at him, ugh, I said as I brushed past him.

He grabbed my arm and slung me in the dressing room, closing the door behind him.

What the fuc-

Ssshhhh, he interrupted me placing a finger to my mouth.

I smacked his finger away from my mouth, don't put your nasty ass finger on my mouth, I snapped.

You miss me, he said reaching out to touch my stomach.

I smacked his hand away, miss you? I can't stand your bitch ass, now move the fuck out my way, I snapped tryna walk past him he grabbed my arm, and pushed me into the wall.

I need you to do something for me, he said serious ass hell.

Fuck I look like, I don't even fuck with you like that, now get the fuck out my way, I semi yelled pushing him.

He grabbed me again, and pushed me into the wall harder, he pulled out a gun, and stuck it in my face.

This ain't no favor, bitch it's a demand, he said tighten his grip around the gun.

Fuck him I know he's not stupid enough to shoot me in a crowded ass mall.

I hawked spit in his face, fuck you.

He laughed, and used his free hand to wipe his face with his shirt. He pulled out his phone and called a number, putting it on speaker.

Yea, a male voice answered the phone.

That bitch ass nigga in the car with you, he asked the guy on the phone.

Yeah, hold on, the guy said.

Hello, I heard Kai voice.

Ka, I tried to say but as soon as I opened my mouth he stuck his gun in it, tears begin to stream down my face.

Hello, is that you lady? Kai questioned, he knows my voice, it want take him long to figure out.

What nigga this Dee, how much you say them things was, he asked him.

My gal around you bra, he asked him.

Naw that was tiff, he lied.

Yea if you say so, they 15, Kai said.

Aight, put dame back on the phone, he said.

Was up, Dame, Dee's brother said.

If his bitch don't wanna corporate, kill him, I'll call you in a few and let you know what she says, he told him, while hanging up the phone.

I tried to speak but my sounds were muffled by the gun.

You say something, he asked taking the gun out my mouth.

What do you need me to do, I said mad as hell.

That's what I thought you said, he said lowering the gun smiling.

Chanel

So he was cool about it when you told him, My best friend Kali said.

Yea, our relationship has actually gotten better since I told him, I said

So he got all this money, why he didn't move his babymama up out of her mama's house, my other friend Leslie said.

I sucked my teeth for some reason Leslie, and I always bumped heads.

He just found out the other day, he might have plans for that, I said to her.

So is he still with that girl, Leslie asked.

Leslie why you always gotta throw salt, I snapped on her.

I'm just being a friend, I told you not to fuck with him in the first place, now you pregnant, and he still with his girl, at least she don't stay with her mama, Leslie said.

Fuck you Leslie, at least he's still around, where is Lawrence daddy, exactly, I said getting frustrated.

Can y'all stop why every time, we get together y'all two gotta go at it, Kali spoke up.

Im just keeping it real, Leslie spoke.

I opened my mouth to say something, but Kali stopped me.

Just let it go, she said.

I sighed, and picked up the phone to send hustla a text saying I was hungry.

I looked up as my lil sister Naomi stuck her head thru the door.

Can you take us to the mall sissy, she asked.

Please, her twin Noel said.

Aight give me 10mins, I said.

I loved my little sisters, and they know I will do anything for them.

Shid I'm going too, Kali said.

We all got up and walked outside, we climbed in my car, and I was about to pull off when I saw hustla car turning in.

Was up y'all, he spoke to everybody in my car.

Hey, they all said.

Where you going, he asked leaning through my window.

The twins wanted to go to the mall, I said.

Um did you eat, he asked.

Not yet, I said.

He dug in his pocket pulling out a knot so big it took him a minute to pull it out. He counted Out seven hundred and gave it to me.

Give the twins a hunnit, he said.

Thank you, the twins said together.

He nodded, no problem, he said to them.

He leaned in and kissed my cheek, call me when you get back, he said before getting in his car pulling off.

Bitchhhh, you got a good one, Kali said smiling.

Don't cuss in front of the twins, I said laughing.

Really were 14, noel the youngest said.

OK sit yo young ass back and shut up, I said pulling off as everyone started laughing.

CHAPTER TWENTY-FIVE

Kai:

I had one arm on the arm rest, and the other on the door, as I rode around listening to Dame talk.

You a fool man, I said laughing at his wack ass joke.

My mind was really on Kayla, I know my baby voice from anywhere, that was her. Lately Dee been on some slick shit, that been my nigga since way back. See I wasn't to heavy into selling drugs, my thing was robbing. If you got it I'm coming to get it. I put Dee on a few years back, when I robbed this nigga that had bricks. I fronted em to Dee, and he flipped it. A couple years ago Dee spot got hit twice, he fell off hard. That was my nigga so I gave him something to get back on his feet. Since he got a fucked up gambling problem, he lost the money quick. A couple months ago he got mad cause I started doing business with Hustla, but that's all it is business, I aint tryna start hanging out with this nigga. Every since then we been distant, till he called me a couple days ago tryna buy work.

I tapped my finger on the door, as he stopped at a stop sign.

I reached down with my left hand putting the car in park, and pulling my strap out with my right, I hit him in the face with my gun repeatedly.

Where the fuck they at, I yelled aiming my gun in his face.

What you talking bout man, he coughed as blood came out.

Don't fuck with me Dame, y'all niggas thought I was stupid huh, I'm the brains in the click, how the fuck y'all gone try to out smart me, I yelled smacking him again.

Drive this muthafucka, I yelled sticking the gun to his neck.

I can't see man, its blood in my eyes, he cried.

Drive! I don't give a fuck bitch you betta squint, I said smacking him again.

I looked in the back for something to wipe his face with, it was a lot of blood on it.

Take me wherever they at, I said giving him a shirt to wipe his face.

Leslie:

After leaving the mall we went back to Chanel's. I can't believe she got pregnant by Hustla, all the girls at our old school wanted him including me. I listened to her go on and on about him, but she can keep talking, I will have my day with him.

Are you still going with me to the party, I asked Kali.

What party, Chanel asked.

My cousin Marco is throwing his girl a surprise party Saturday, I said.

Damn bitch you didn't invite me, she said.

What are you gonna do at a party pregnant, I asked her.

I'm not even showing, she stated.

Well the party is Saturday, were meeting up at my house by seven, I told her.

I looked down at my vibrating phone, it was my grandma so I knew it was time to pick up Lawrence. I said my good bye's before leaving, I pulled up at my grandma house 30 mins later.

Hey mama, my three year old son said.

Hey dink you been good for grandma today, I asked while kissing his cheek.

Yes, now where is my candy, he asked smiling.

I got you kid, I said walking towards the back to speak to my grandma.

After getting home, I fed and bathed him, and we cuddled on the couch to watch ninja turtles. I loved my son, but I hated this single parent life, Larry my sons father came around every blue moon. He says he don't like to come because of where I lived, but if you wanted to be apart of your son's life wouldn't nothing stop you, not even coming in the projects.

I begin to doze off when I heard a knock at the door.

Was up trick, I said opening the door for my girl pinky.

Was up, she said taking a seat on the empty couch.

Nothing, I said while taking sleeping Lawrence to his room.

You know who asked about you today, she said smiling.

I sucked my teeth cause I already knew who she was talking bout.

Who, I asked anyway.

Quick, she said passing me a rello to break down.

So bitch I told you I don't want him, I said aggravated.

Quick, was a known drug dealer around the projects. He's been tryna holla at me since I moved in, but I wouldn't give him the time of day.

Plus I got my eye on someone else, I said blushing.

He don't have Quick's money, she said.

I laughed, you right he don't have Quick's money, his money shitin on Quick's.

Who, she asked confused.

His name is Hustla, I said blushing harder.

From out west, she asked getting excited.

Yea, how you know him, I asked her.

Who don't know his fine ass, she said laughing.

Slow yo roll bitch, he's mine, I stated, as we both laughed.

I got up to get my phone charger, before realizing I left it in the car.

Was up Leslie, I heard a male voice call out.

I turned around to be face to face with Quick.

Don't get me wrong Quick was fine, and had money, but I was determined to get some of Hustla. Quick is somebody I would make my dude, so I had to get some of hustla, before even considering talking to Quick.

Was up Quick, I said back.

What you up to girl, he asked standing beside me.

Nothing just chilling, I said.

Can I come chill with you, he asked.

I shot him a look, I bet you do a lot of chilling with girls around here, I said.

He laughed, so is that a yes or no.

Not tonight, I have work in the morning, I said.

When are you free, can I take you out, he asked stepping closer to me, he smelled so good.

Um sure I would like that, I said blushing.

So you gone give me your number, he said pulling out his phone.

I put it in, and I gave it back to him.

Yo Quick, a guy called from down the sidewalk.

He held up his finger, then turned to me, ima call you aight.

OK, I said turning to walk away. He grabbed my arm, and pulled me into a hug. Wrapping his arms around my waist, it shocked me, I didn't know what to do so I put my arms around his neck.

You gone be mine, he whispered in my ear.

He slipped his hand down to my ass but I moved it breaking away, we'll see, I said turning to walk in the house.

You smell like chicken, and I want some, he said as he walked down the sidewalk. I couldn't do nothing but laugh, since I fried chicken for Lawrence earlier, and haven't showered yet.

When I got back inside, me and pinky talked a little longer, then she left. I jumped in the shower, lotioned up, and laid down. I was sleep for about a hour when my phone rung.

Hello, I answered.

Can I come get that plate, a male voice said.

I laughed as I looked at the phone to see what time it was.

Its one in the morning, I said.

I'm hungry, open the door, he said.

I hung up, grabbed my robe, and went downstairs to open the door.

He walked in looking high ass hell. I shut the door and locked it as he observed my apartment.

Nice crib, he said sitting on the couch comfortably.

I just smiled and walked to the kitchen to heat his plate up. I bet he thought it was nice cause most of these girls over here got bugs for days, bad ass kids running around with their diapers touching the ground. My grandma don't play that shit, she will call DCS on me.

Ayee, Leslie can I use yo bathroom, he asked walking towards me.

Yes, its upstairs first door on the right, and please don't wake my son, I said.

I ain't girl, he said walking off.

He sat on the couch with his plate, I sat beside him. I watched him as he said his grace, and tasted the food. Once he saw it was good he started to fuck it up.

You gone watch me or talk to me, he said putting Macaroni in his mouth.

I laughed, what do you wanna talk about.

You, he said biting his chicken.

What about me, I said blushing.

Where yo man at, he asked.

If I had one you wouldn't be here, I said taking his empty plate from him.

I sat back down handing him something to drink, he took a couple sips and sat it down. He grabbed me pulling me closer.

You smell good, he said.

Thanks,

If I'm late for work tomorrow ima kick your ass, I said.

I'm not gone let you be late, I just need a minute of your time, he said licking his lips.

I'm not like the rest of these ho's over here Quick, I said.

I know that, that's why I respect you Leslie, I like you, I've been chasing you for what like a year now, and I'm just now getting close to you, he said rubbing my thigh.

I just looked at him, he gently grabbed my chin, and kissed me. His kiss felt perfect, and real, it sent chills down my spine.

Quick I can't, I said pulling away.

He bit down on his lip, and just looked at me, his phone rung drawing his attention.

I gotta go, he said standing up.

I walked him to the door, he pulled me into a hug, grabbing my ass. This time I didn't stop him I was a little more comfortable.

Call me tomorrow, he said kissing my cheek, and leaving.

I went to sleep that night with a smile.

CHAPTER TWENTY-SIX

Kayla:

This nigga wanted me to show him where my cousin stay. Why was he so obsessed with her, we pulled up to the house I showed him.

See they're not home, I lied I knew damn well this wasn't their house.

Can I go now? I asked getting frustrated.

Naw we got another stop to make, he said getting on the interstate.

We pulled up to an abandoned house.

Whats here Dell take me back now, I yelled.

He snatched me out the car by my hair, pulling me inside.

Dame, he called out for his brother.

He didn't answer, we walked down a long hallway, to a set of stairs.

Go, he demanded.

My heart was pounding with each step I took.

Go bitch, he said as he pushed me when I got down to the second to last step. I stumbled into the dark, I felt somebody grab me, and gently pull me to the side. It was Kai I knew that cologne from anywhere. He snatched Dell down the rest of the steps and started beating him. He punched him repeatedly with his fist, and when he got tired of using his fist, he started to stomp him. Blood gushed out from every part of his body.

That's enough Kailin you're going to kill him, I said grabbing Kai's arm.

He looked at me and pulled me into a hug.

You alright lady, he asked me.

I wanna go home, I said.

We left Dell there to suffer and went home.

Yotti:

Why don't y'all move in your daddy's old house, its big enough, and empty, aunt Chell said.

I never thought about it, it would feel weird being there without Mell, and my daddy.

Do you have the keys? I asked her as I walked towards the back door.

Yeah, hold on, she said going downstairs to get them.

After leaving my auntie house, I called Hustle to tell him to meet me there. I pulled up in the driveway, the grass was so high you couldn't see the front porch from the street. I grabbed boss out the car, and walked up the walk way to the front porch. I walked inside, and everything that was once there was gone. Boss begin to roam around, I closed the front door and begin to do the same. I walked thru the living room Then the kitchen, my attention was stuck on the kitchen window, I heard the front door open and close.

Baby, Langston called out.

I walked around to the front door. He wrapped his arms around me kissing me.

Wats up with this, he asked looking around the living room.

It's ours, come on let's look around, I said pulling his arm.

You look cute, Kayla said walking into my room.

thanks boo, so do you, I said as I applied eye shadow.

It was Saturday and we were getting ready for the party. Boss was with auntie, and Langston is going to meet me there. After MyMy, and Lola finally pulled up, we got into Kayla's car and headed to the party. The parking lot was packed, MyMy thought we were just going out, she didn't know Marco had rented the place out for her.

IDs please, the bouncer said.

I dug in my clutch hoping that this fake ID Langston gave me worked.

Turn around, he said once examining the ID.

They let us through we opened the doors, and as soon as we walked in everybody yelled surprise.

Aight y'all the birthday girl is in the house, fellas let's past them drinks and get this party crackin, the Dj yelled, as the music dropped.

Marco walked up hugging MyMy, y'all in VIP, he said leading the way.

We sat on the plush red couches, as three waitresses came out with bottles with sparks flying everywhere. They begin to pour up, and bounce to the music. I looked over and saw Langston in the corner talking to Kai. I tapped Kayla and stood up, she stood up behind me. I headed his way as a girl approached him, she was all in his face.

I'm good shawty, I could hear him tell her when I got closer.

Hey daddy, I said brushing past the girl to hug Langston.

Wasup girl, he said wrapping his arms around me gripping my ass.

The girl sucked her teeth and walked off.

C'mere girl, what you got on, he said pulling me closer gripping my ass with one hand and rubbing his other hand up my thigh.

I could tell he had already been drinking and was high as fuck. I looked over at Kayla who was hugged up with Kai. I felt his index finger glide across my pearl, I jumped a little.

Stop Langston, it's a room full of people, I said looking around, and backing up a little.

So, you mine fuck what anybody say, he said pulling me closer, sticking his hand back in my panties.

Chanel:

The party was live, we followed Leslie to the VIP section, to speak to her cousin.

Wasup Marco, she said giving him a hug.

Wasup, he said to her.

She turned to some girl sitting beside him, and wished her a happy birthday, I'm assuming that's his girlfriend.

These are my girls Kali, and Chanel, she said introducing us.

Hey, we both spoke.

I looked at the other girl that was with the girlfriend, and she looked really familiar, but I couldn't place her.

Y'all can chill up here cuz, let me know if y'all need something, Marco said before walking into the crowd.

Leslie sat down and started to make conversation with his girlfriend. I nodded my head to the music, when I noticed Hustla in the corner with some girl.

Yo ain't that your baby daddy, Kali said spotting him to.

Yep, I said as I sat there and watched him.

I got the courage to get up and go over there, with Kali right behind me. When I got closer the girl lifted her head laughing, that's when I realized it was his girl. His eyes locked with mine, as I walked past them to the restroom. The bathroom line was really long, and I really had to pee, so I asked the bartender if they had another bathroom. He pointed behind the stage, I nodded and went, glade nobody but us was in there I rushed to the cleanest stall.

Did you see the way he looked at me? I called to Kali, as I opened my stall door.

What are you doing here? I asked him as he stood over me.

Naw what you are doing here? he asked while pushing me into the stall locking the door.

Don't ask me shit, with your girlfriend out there, I said with an attitude, I hated seeing them two together.

He reached out and grabbed the top of my dress, pulling my Breast out, he cupped them before placing one in his mouth. My knees felt weak, as he begin to massage my pearl with his free hand. He stepped back and looked at me, he sat down on the toilet seat pulling his stick out. He gripped my waist pulling me towards him, he lifted my dress, and slid my panties off, while pulling me in his lap. I wrapped my arms around his neck as I felt him enter me.

Damn you so wet, he moaned as I rotated my hips on him, clinching my pussy muscles.

You like that daddy, I said as I rode him.

Hell yeah, he said gripping my waist tighter.

Stand up, he said while slapping my ass.

I did as he said and bent over the toilet as he stroked deep from behind, a few minutes later he got his nut and we cleaned off. Kali and I walked back to the VIP section, and I almost chocked when I saw hustla's girl there talking to the birthday girl, this can't be real.

CHAPTER TWENTY-SEVEN

Four months later.

Yotti:

I sat in my office at home doing my homework. Langston was at class and boss was taking a nap. We had gotten settled in daddy's old house about a Month ago. A knock at the front door caught my attention.

Hey boo, I spoke as I opened the door for Lola.

I knew something was wrong because her eyes were red, and puffy.

Wats wrong, I asked locking the door, and pulling her into a hug.

I can't take it no more, she cried on my shoulder.

What happened, I asked pulling her to the bathroom.

I tried to help her, but she went off on me saying keep my hands off her man, she said between sobs.

Lola's stepdad beats on them, I guess she's finally had enough.

It's OK Lo you can stay with me as long as you need to, I said wiping tears off her face.

After calming her down we sat in the den and watched TV.

So, what are you naming her, she said rubbing my now showing belly.

Lexington Yatise, I said with a smile.

That's pretty, did you do your English paper, she asked.

I nodded my head and got up to get it. We chilled the rest of the night, till we got ready for school the next day.

Leslie

I flipped thru a magazine at work, we were slow today and I was bored as hell.

I'm going to take my 15, I told my coworker Tamia.

I walked in the back pulling out my phone calling Quick, We have gotten closer these last four months.

Was up baby, he said answering the phone.

Hey what you are doing, I asked.

Thinking about you, he said, which caused me to blush.

We talked a little while before I heard Tamia call my name for help.

I need this in a 1x, I heard someone say.

When I turned the corner and saw Hustla looking thru the shirts, my stomach started to do flips. I thought dealing with Quick would get my mind off of wanting Hustla, but I guess not.

You need help finding anything, I walked beside him and said.

He looked me up and down and licked his lips.

Yeah, can I get a 2x, he said holding up the shirt.

Hustla

She walked towards the back and I couldn't help but glance at her ass. I quickly shook it off, and walked towards Kai, and the other cashier, she was fine ass fuck.

I think that color looks great on you, she said to Kai.

Hey how you doing, I asked her walking up to them.

She blushed, showing them pretty white teeth, I'm fine and you, she asked.

I'm good, I said licking my lips causing her to blush harder.

Here you go, the other girl came from the back and said.

Thank you, I said while taking the shirt from her.

I didn't get your name, I said turning my attention back to the other girl.

That's cause I didn't give it to you, she smirked.

Tamia, I said reading her name tag, I'm Hustla, I said extending my hand to her.

Nice meeting you, she said shaking my hand, and turning her attention towards Kai.

Can you assist me over here, I asked the other girl.

Is there a special occasion, she asked as we got to the back of the store.

Nah, its just my birthday in a couple of days, I said scanning thru the shirts.

Are you doing anything special, she asked me.

Nah I'm just chilling that day, I told her.

Why you should always celebrate your birthday, you never know which one could be your last, she said looking me up and down.

Wats yo name, I asked her.

Leslie, she said blushing.

Kayla:

Kai made me promise not to say anything about the Dell situation, he said he would take care of it so I left it alone. MyMy and I were at the Mexican restaurant having drinks. We got away with everything with these fake IDs.

Marco's been really distant lately, she said referring to her boyfriend.

What do you mean? I asked taking a bite from my tacos.

Marco always makes time for me, lately he's been to busy, she said sipping her margarita.

Y'all don't still argue like you were at first right, I asked her.

She shot me a look, its worse, I can't even ask him about the baby, or why the girl called my phone and said that without him going off.

A girl walked in carrying a baby, I smiled because I wanted a baby, but Kai don't think its time. The waitress seated her two booths down from us, MyMy back was facing her so she couldn't see. I turned my attention back to MyMy, when out the corner of my eye I saw a guy sit in the booth with her. I had to double look before realizing it was Marco. MyMy must have saw me because she turned to look to.

What the fuck, she said standing up.

MyMy please be cordial in here, I said grabbing her arm.

Okay, she said sucking her teeth.

A waitress sat a pitcher at their table and walked off as MyMy walked up.

What's this Marco? she asked approaching them.

Marco looked stuck like he seen a ghost.

Who are you, she said turning to the girl.

I'm his girl who are you, she asked MyMy.

Naw you not my gal, Marco said collecting his thoughts.

Baby it's not what it look like, he tried to explain himself.

MyMy picked up the whole pitcher, and dumped it on his head, fuck you Marco, and your family, she said before looking at me, let's go Kayla, she said walking out the door. I thru 40 dollars on the table and left.

MyMy:

I couldn't stop the tears from rolling down my face. How could he do this to me, I asked him all he had to do was tell the truth. Kayla dropped me off at home, I laid down and cried as my mind drifted off to the past.

I've known Marco since kindergarten, he was always so quiet and distant from everybody, we stayed two houses down from each other. One day when we were 8, he walked up to me as I was outside playing, he said something so low I could barely hear him.

Can you speak up a little I can't hear you, I said moving closer to him.

He looked at me with those pretty brown eyes and said, do y'all have some noodles.

Huh, sure, I said sneaking in the house getting him some noodles. We've been cool ever since that day.

One day when we were 10, I saw him sitting on the porch sad.

Hey Marco, I said sitting beside him.

He spoke dryly without looking at me, what's wrong, I asked him as he looked down at his busted-up shoes.

Nothing, he mumbled.

Yes, it is, if you tell me I will sneak you some macaroni, I said scooting closer to him I knew macaroni was his favorite.

Foreal, he said looking at me with a huge smile.

Yeah, I said smiling back.

He sighed, I'm just tired of this, I'm tired of asking you for food, I'm tired of my brother and sister running off leaving me to fiend for myself, today is food stamp day, and we don't have no food why because my trifling mother's drug habit comes before her kids, he said looking like he wanted to cry.

It's okay Marco, I will be here for you, I said wrapping my arms around him.

I was lying in bed when I heard a tap at my window, I got up to unlock it knowing it was Marco. Ever since that day he opened up to me about his mama I've been there for him. He crawled through with a busted lip, and black eye.

What happened Marco, I whispered so no one could hear us.

Mama got caught tryna steal out off her boyfriend's pocket, and he beat our ass, he said sitting on the bed.

I left out of the room to get him a hot rag, I gave it to him and crawled back in bed. He dabbed at his lip before stripping down to his boxers climbing beside me.

I love you Mylasia, he said into my ear.

I love you too, I whispered scooting closer to him.

We were now 12, Marco hated being at home, so he's been sneaking in my window since we were 10. This night was no different from the rest, until he stuck his hand in my panties.

Stop Marco, I giggled moving his hand.

Let me touch you, he said doing it again, and I let him.

Kayla was right he did pop my cherry at 12, I let him because I believed him when he said I was the only one for him, and that he was mine and I was his, I believed it so much that it never bothered me to see him with other females, because I knew he belonged to me, now he has a baby by someone else.

The sound of my window sliding up snapped me out of my thoughts. I didn't turn to look because I knew it was Marco. We were now 18 and Marco has come a long way he replaced his busted shoes for Jordan's, his high waters for true religion, I must say tho that once he got on his feet he made sure I was straight. He stripped to his boxers and climbed in beside me. He pulled me close to him, I kept my back turned towards him, as tears ran down my cheek.

I'm sorry baby, he said holding me tight.

I asked you Marco, you told me you didn't know her, I said between sobs.

I don't know her, it happened one time baby, he said turning me to face him.

And you didn't think to wear a rubber, I said looking into eyes.

I did, it broke, she doesn't mean nothing to me it was a mistake, I was drunk, he said wiping tears off my face.

So how you know she's yours, I said.

I got a blood test, I will never hurt you like that again Mylasia, but I have to take care of my daughter, he said to me.

I just looked at him, I didn't know what to say, but I did know that I loved Marco, and I wasn't ready to let him go, I wrapped my arms around him laying my head on his chest.

I love you girl, he said.

I love you to, I said kissing his lips

CHAPTER TWENTY EIEGHT

Yotti:

I hoped in my car leaving school, I drove a few blocks to pick boss up from school. Langston's birthday was coming up, and I had no idea of what to do for him. I pulled up at the house, and there was a woman standing on my porch.

Hi, may I help you, I asked as I approached the porch.

You must be Maurice, she said smiling and gently pinched boss cheek.

I slightly pulled him back, I didn't know this woman, I turned to see Langston's car pulling in the driveway.

I'm sorry I'm Dominic, she said extending her hand.

Her name sounded familiar, but I couldn't place it.

I'm sorry ma'am I don't believe I know you, I said ready to get inside I had to use it.

I'm Melanie's sister, she spoke.

The one she didn't like I thought to myself.

Wasup baby, Langston said climbing the steps, and kissing my lips.

Hey, I said.

How you doing? he said to Dominic, as he grabbed boss out of my arms and went inside.

She spoke back, can we go inside to talk, she asked me.

No, we'll talk here, I said taking a seat on one of the chairs, she followed suit.

I'm sorry I didn't get your name, she said.

Yotti, I calmly stated.

OK um Yotti, I know we haven't formally met, but I'm Melanie's older sister, I came by here a few months back, and this place was empty, I didn't know someone had moved in, she said.

So, if you thought it was still vacant why did you come, I asked ready to get to the point.

Who are you, she asked.

I'm Melanie's stepdaughter, I said.

She sucked her teeth, well my mother and I came by here a few months back and the house looked abandoned, since this was my sisters place, my mother has all rights to it, and she thought it would be best if I stayed here and kept the place up.

I slightly laughed, you're right someone needs to be here to keep it up, but I have it covered now, I said standing to leave.

See you don't understand MS Yotti, since my sister is gone, this house belongs to my mother, I understand that you are here, so were willing to give you a month to leave, it was nice meeting you, she said leaving.

Who the fuck this bitch think she is, I thought, I followed her, and stopped her at her car.

Are you serious? I said.

Dead ass, she said with a smirk.

My mom didn't even fuck with y'all, I don't remember seeing any of y'all at her funeral, I don't remember any of y'all there when she had my brother except for Monica, she didn't want you here when she was alive, so you're damn sure not gonna be here while she's dead, I spoke before turning to walk in the house.

Whatever you say little girl, like I said you have one month, she said.

Please don't underestimate me because I'm young, you brought your ass to my house, you have never seen your "nephew" and you could give two shits about him you haven't asked how he's doing or nothing, but can fix your mouth to ask to stay here, she may be Melanie's mother but this is my house, if you would have come to the will reading you would know she gave it to me, so miss me with the bullshit, and get the fuck off my property, I yelled she has officially pissed me off.

You aight baby, Langston asked walking outside, wrapping his arms around my waist.

I'm fine she was just leaving, I said as she sucked her teeth, climbed in her car and left.

I walked inside, and rushed to the bathroom, my nerves were literally on ten.

What was that about, Langston asked standing in the door.

After filling him in, boss and I went to the store so I could cook, when I got back Lola was there.

Was up, where is Langston, I asked her.

He left not too long ago, he said he'd be back before the food is ready, she said playing with boss.

I sat the groceries down and washed my hands so I could prepare the food.

Did you hear about Dee? Lola asked.

I sucked my teeth, what about him, I said.

He's missing, she said.

What do you mean missing? I said turning to face her.

No one has seen him they reported him missing, she said.

I don't know why but I felt dizzy, my mind was racing, did Langston have something to do with this, I can't deal with him going to jail for murder. I leaned against the sink, as I felt nauseated.

You OK, Lola asked me.

Water please, I got out as I breathed heavily tryna keep from throwing up.

I need to lay down for a min, I said taking small sips from my water bottle.

Go ahead, I'll finish dinner, and I got boss, she said handing him a cookie.

As soon as my head hit the pillow, I fell asleep.

Hustla

I was in the car with Kai, looking thru my insta, when a DM popped up. I looked at it and laughed, it was the Leslie girl from the store, she sent me her number, so I called.

Hello, she answered.

Was up, I said to her.

Who is this?

Hustla, I said.

Awww hey was up with you, she said

Nothing just chillin, I said.

Oh, can I chill with you, she said.

I looked at the phone and laughed, naw I'm good, but I do need you to do something for me, I said.

What, she asked.

Give me that girl number, that work with you, Tamia, I said.

She caught a major attitude, I'm not no fucking match maker, I didn't give you my number to get you on with the next bitch, she snapped.

I hope you didn't think I was gonna fuck with you, you cool with my babymama, I said laughing.

She hung straight up; fuck her I can get gal number myself.

We pulled up at the spot, Kai and I had been doing good business together, he wasn't that bad, so we became cool.

What day that shipment coming in? I asked juju as I flopped on the couch beside him.

Thursday, at 3a.m, he said taking a pull from his blunt.

Cool, you and gutta gone handle it, I asked taking the blunt from him.

Naw Gutta got something else to do, we got a new problem he is working on, you gotta be there, he said.

I can't I got shit to do, I said.

I'll go, Kai spoke up.

What, nigga I don't know you like that, juju said.

I saw Kai getting mad, so I spoke up.

Chill out Ju, my nigga cool people, I turned to Kai, you gone go foreal, I asked.

Yeah, I'll go, he said.

Cool, we set so let's dip, I said standing dapping juju up, and leaving with Kai behind me.

You know I'm putting my trust into you, I said to Kai as we pulled off.

Chill my nigga I got chu, he said.

CHAPTER TWENTY-NINE

Chanel:

I was laying down when hustla called me, telling me to meet him somewhere. I pulled up at the address, climbed out and walked to his car.

Please don't take long I have work in a few, I said to him as I walked up.

Damn was up, I can't get a greeting first, he said climbing out the car.

I just sucked my teeth, as he reached out and pulled me into a hug, he smelled so good, his hand gripped my ass. I tried to pull back, but he gripped me tighter.

What's wrong cha, you don't love daddy nomo, he said in my ear.

I sighed heavily, why are we here, I asked him.

Wats yo problem Chanel, you been really distant lately, he said letting me go.

He was right, I have distance myself from him, I was tired of playing the sideline role. I know when I first started talking to him, he told me about her, but that gets old. When I heard rumors that he moved her into a big as house it really drew the line for me. The last time I saw him was at the party, I've been dodging him.

I don't have a problem, now why are we here, I asked him.

So why I ain't heard from you in four months, he said sounding frustrated.

You have a girlfriend so why do you care about my whereabouts, I said with a smirk.

He just starred at me, then turned to walk towards the house.

Come on girl, he said once he noticed I was still standing there.

I walked behind him on the porch, as he stuck a key in opening the door. The house was beautiful, and fully furnished. It was a three bedroom, and two bath houses, it wasn't big but it wasn't small either it was just right.

Why are we here? I asked looking around the living room.

He held the keys up, dangling them in my face.

What are you saying Langston? I said hoping he was saying what I think he is saying.

I'm saying my baby needs its space, he said rubbing my big belly.

A huge smile was on my face as I jumped in his arms wrapping my legs around his waist.

Thank you, daddy I love, you sooo much, I said as I planted kisses all over his face.

Aw so now I'm daddy, I love you to girl, he said kissing my lips for the very first time. Hustla made it clear to me from jump that he doesn't kiss nobody but his girl, but he just kissed me.

Go look at the house, he said putting me down.

I walked around looking at all the rooms. One room had two full sized beds in there, and it was decorated in purple and zebra, for the twins, the other room was empty, and the master bedroom had a king size bed, a fireplace, a connected bathroom, and walk in closet.

Since you been dodging me, I didn't know what you were having, so I left the baby room for you to decorate, he said while standing in the doorway of the master bedroom.

I walked towards him and pulled him in the room, I stood on my tippy toes, and kissed his lips, he slipped his tongue in my mouth, as he picked me up carrying me to the bed, Damn I love this nigga.

Leslie:

I laughed as Quick held me down tickling me.

Please stop I can't breathe, I got out between laughs.

If you gone stop playing with me, he asked still holding me down.

Yes, I quit, I said as he let me up.

Quick and I made it official a month ago. When I first introduced him to Lawrence, they hit it off, so it made me consider making him my man. Quick spoils the shit out of him, everything he ask for Quick gets it for him. He knows the situation between me and Larry, he said fuck Larry Lawrence gone be straight regardless. I climbed out the bed, to answer the door, I wanted to shut the door back when I saw who it was.

What Larry, I said standing in the doorway.

Fuck you mean what, where my son, he asked pushing me out the way walking inside.

He's taking a nap, if you would have called before you came you would have known that I said with my hand on my hip.

Whatever go wake him up, he said waving me off.

No, he just went to sleep, you can come back later, I said walking towards the door opening it.

Girl if you don't go get my son, he semi yelled.

Why so you can spend 10 mins with him and leave, it's funny you always say my son but don't do shit for him, Larry you can leave with that bullshit, I said getting frustrated.

Look bitch I ain't in the mood to play with you, he yelled getting in my face.

I kill niggas that disrespect me, Quick said coming downstairs.

Larry looked at him confused, who the fuck is you, he said.

It doesn't matter you heard what I said when you disrespect my girl you disrespect me, and I'm zero tolerance on disrespect, so you owe her an apology, Quick said.

Who the fuck is he, Larry asked looking at me.

He's my boyfriend, he just told you that, now I said Lawrence is sleep you can come back later, I said getting frustrated.

You be having this nigga around my son, Larry asked looking at me.

Your son, nigga I been around the last five months, and I've never seen you come check on him, I've never seen you call to see how he's doing, everything that Lil boy needs I get for him, so you can move around with all that, matter of fact, Quick paused as he opened the door, grabbed Larry by his shirt, and literally thru him out, don't bring yo ass back around here, if you do I guarantee you want make it out these projects alive, he said before closing the door.

Can you do me a favor, he asked in a whole different tone then just a second ago.

What, I asked as he sat down, pulling me in his lap.

Please keep his bitch ass away from over here, he said.

I didn't know, he stopped me from finishing my sentence.

Just say OK baby, he said.

OK, I said as I leaned down to kiss his lips.

Chanel:

You gone go get the stuff for the baby today, hustla asked me as he begin putting his clothes back on.

I guess since you made me call out today, I can got get her stuff, I said holding the covers around my naked body.

Her? You are having a girl, he asked.

Yes, what do you think I should name her, I asked him.

Alexis, he said after he thought for a minute.

Alexis Chanel, I like that, I said.

Aight I gotta go, he said.

He dug in his pocket and pulled out a credit card.

Use this to get whatever else you need for the house, I'll be back a Lil later, he said as he bent down to kiss my lips, and he left.

I couldn't help the huge smile that sat on my face, I called Kali, and told her to come over. I showered and got dressed, as I waited till, she came, I got up to open the door for her.

Bitch what was so important, she asked as she walked in looking around.

You like, I asked as I closed and locked the door.

This you, she asked shocked.

Yep, hustla gave me the keys today, I said.

You go girl, she said as we both laughed.

Show me the rest of the house, she said walking around.

After I finished giving her a tour, we left to shop for the baby, I paid a guy from the store to come over and put all the furniture up for me. Kali helped me paint her room, then we went to mamas to get my stuff from there. Good thing mama was gone, but the twins were there.

I begin to pack all my clothes with Kali's help.

Where you going, Noel barged in my room asking me.

I'm moving, I said without looking up.

Moving where, Naomi said sitting on my bed.

I have my own place the baby and I need our own space, I said as I begin to carry bags downstairs to the car.

Why are you just now telling us? Noel said following me.

Noel I'm the big sister not you, I tell you when I feel like telling you, I said going into the house to get more bags.

Can we go with you? Naomi asked coming down the stairs with some bags.

I'll have to come back there's no room, I said loading the last of my stuff in the car.

Yotti:

Langston's birthday was tomorrow, and I've finally came up with what I wanted to do. Boss was at aunties for the weekend, I sat at home patiently waiting on my surprise delivery to come. I told Langston he couldn't come home till nine, and it was seven, I was frustrated because the people were supposed to be here at 6:30. I walked into the kitchen to start our dinner, I stuck the steaks in the oven, when my doorbell rang.

Hello, we have a delivery for Yatise Hernandez, the delivery man said.

Yes, that's me, will you guys set it up for me, I asked letting the two men inside.

Sure, we just need a signature here, and a place to put it, he said.

I signed the form and led them to where I wanted them to set it up. I walked back into the kitchen to finish dinner as they set up Langston's surprise.

CHAPTER THRITY

Hustla:

I laid on the couch watching TV, with Chanel up under me. She begins to doze off as I rubbed her stomach, when the doorbell rang.

Was up, I said to Kali, and Leslie as I opened the door.

Hey, both said.

She in the living room, I said as I turned and walked towards the room.

This nice, I heard Leslie tell her.

Thanks boo, she said.

I looked at my watch to see if it was going on nine, I slipped my shoes on, and went in the living room to tell cha I was finna leave, when I heard Leslie say something slick.

So now you got the house, how long is it gone take him to leave his girl, she said.

Leslie don't start, I could hear Kali tell her.

What? I'm just saying, Leslie said shrugging her shoulders.

I'm finna go cha, I said as I bent down to kiss her lips.

OK I love you, she said.

I love you to girl, I said as I turned to walk off.

Did you still need her number? Leslie said as I opened the front door.

I stopped in my tracks; I know this bitch ain't tryna be funny in my house.

Who the fuck you talking to, I snapped.

You, did you get Tamia's number, she asked with a smirk.

What is she talking about hustla, Chanel said as she stood up from the couch.

My jaws begin to Flench, and my temples begin to throb.

Bitch what the fuck is you talking about, I asked walking towards her, I wanted to smack that bitch.

What are you talking about Leslie? Chanel asked her.

He came in my job one day, and was tryna talk to Tamia, he asked me for her number, but I told him that you were my friend, and I wasn't tryna get in the middle of that, she told Chanel.

Bitch you a lie, why the fuck would I ask you for her number when I know you cool with my babymama, I yelled this bitch was pissing me off.

She opened her mouth to say something, but I stopped her. I snatched her off the couch by her hair causing her to fall on her ass hard. I drug her to the front door, as she kicked and punched trying to get me to let her go.

Bitch you just a hater, you got to get the fuck up outta here, I yelled.

Let her go hustla, Kali said as she tried to get my hands out of her hair.

Baby please stop, Chanel said pulling on my arm.

Get that funky bitch out my house, I said as I let her go.

You got the right one ol bitch ass nigga, Chanel it want be long before he starts beating your ass, since he so quick to put his hands on a female, Leslie yelled as she tried to charge me but Kali stopped her.

Go get whoever bitch, you know where I be at, I told her as Kali got her out the house, and in the car, they sped off.

I turned to walk out the door, but Chanel grabbed my shirt.

What is she talking about Langston, she asked as tears rolled down her face.

You believe her, as much as she hate on you, and throw salt on you, you gone stand in my face and believe her, I said.

The bitch is mad cause I didn't give her no play, that's the real reason, I said.

She just looked at me.

What you don't believe me, I asked as I pulled out my phone to show her the DM.

I'm sorry Langston, she said once she saw that I was telling the truth.

She wrapped her arms around me and kissed my lips, I love you soo much, she said.

Yeah, I gotta go, I don't want her here no more, cha and I mean that, I said walking out the door, I was pissed off.

Yotti

I piled steak, shrimp, asparagus, and baked potatoes, on two plates. I lit the two candles that sat on the table, and grabbed the wine out the freezer, and sat it in the bucket of ice. I hooked my phone up to the jam box and let Pandora play. I walked in my room pulling off my robe letting my lingerie show, I slipped into my red bottoms, and sat at the table waiting. I glanced at the time when I heard the front door open. Although I didn't get finished till nine thirty, I told this nigga to be here at nine and its ten.

Baby, he called from the front door.

I'm in here, I yelled, not wanting him to see my surprise just yet.

I smelled his cologne, before he even appeared, which made a smile instantly appear on my face.

Damn was up sexy, he said bending down to kiss me.

Hey daddy, I said as I poured both of us a glass of wine.

You look good girl, he said sitting in the seat across from me.

He said his grace, and dug in his food, we talked over dinner, then I led him to the bedroom.

Damn bae what's this, he said laughing and pointing at the stripper pole I had installed.

Your surprise, sit down so I can show you how it works.

Wait you finna strip for me, he asked standing up.

Yes, I said smiling.

Wait, he said walking to the closet, He came back with a stack of 100's.

I begin to dance as drake shut it down, played. He watched me while licking his lips as he threw 100 dollar bills out. That night when we did it, it was different from any other night. He touched, and made love to me, like it was our very first time.

The next morning, we woke up and went to breakfast. Afterwards we met Kayla, Kai, Lola, and gutta at the bowling alley.

Wea that money at, so I can take it, come on run it, gutta said wanting to bet on the bowling game.

Run it then, drop it in my baby's hands, Langston said counting out five hundred, handing it to me.

Gutta, and Kai handed me five hundred each.

Come on baby, let's take they money, Langston said to me kissing my cheek, knowing damn well I can't bowl.

CHAPTER THRITY ONE

Leslie:

I pulled up at the house mad as hell, I brushed past the people outside and went in the house. I looked down at my ringing phone to see Chanel calling, fuck her, and her bitch ass nigga, I thought as I pressed ignore. I was about to call Quick when I heard a knock at the door.

Hey baby, I said opening the door for Quick.

Was up, what's wrong with you, he asked walking in sitting on the couch.

I told him the whole story word from word.

So that nigga put his hands on you, and called you a bitch, he asked sounding pissed.

Yes, I said.

Who the fuck is Chanel's boyfriend? he asked.

This dude name hustla, I said.

From out west, he asked.

Yeah.

Don't worry about it Ima take care of that, he said.

One month later

Yotti

Auntie was having girl's night at her house. We were sitting around eating pizza and playing games.

My babies on her way out, ain't she, MyMy said rubbing my stomach.

Yes girl, and I can't wait, I said laughing, and taking a sip of my juice.

Let's play spades, Kayla called out holding a deck of cards.

I'll pass, MyMy said pulling out her phone.

I don't know how to play, Lola said.

Come on Nyla me, and you vs auntie, and Kayla, I said.

We sat down and begin to play. We were winning at first, but then they set us, causing them to come back and win the game. I pulled out my phone to call Langston, his phone went straight to voicemail.

Hey, have you talked to gutta, I asked Lola.

Naw not since earlier, she said.

Kayla, have you talked to Kai, I called out to her.

Yeah, he's on his way over, why, she asked.

Is Langston with him, I asked.

Nope, she said.

I begin to call his phone over and over again. I called his main line, and his trap line, both were going to voicemail.

Hustla:

I was rushing through traffic, tryna get to the hospital. Chanel called me saying her water broke, and Kali was taking her to the hospital.

How may I help you? the receptionist asked.

I'm here to see Chanel Hughes, I said.

She pointed me in the directions. I tapped on the door, before walking in. Cha was laying down sleeping, and Kali was sitting beside her.

Was up, I spoke to her.

Hey, she said looking up from the tablet she was playing with.

What's going on, I asked Kali as I walked towards Chanel.

They gave her an epidural, the doctor said she would be back in 20 mins to check her cervix, that was 15mins ago, she said looking at the time.

I pulled a chair up to her bed, my phones were ringing nonstop, so I cut them on airplane mode.

Cha, I said gently rubbing her head.

She opened her eyes, but she looked a little high.

Hey baby, she slurred out.

Hello, I'm Dr. Stevens, you must be daddy, she said extending her hand to me.

Yes, how're you doing, I said with a slight grin.

I'm good, you ready to be a daddy, she asked while putting gloves on.

Yes, I'm ready to see my baby girl, I said.

Two hours later, I watched Cha as she held Alexis in her arms. We named her Alexis Chanel Higgins, she weighted 6lb and 13oz. I looked up to see juju, and Kai walk thru the door.

Was up, I said hitting both of em up.

We got a problem, juju said as they pulled me into the hallway.

Quick been running around looking for you, Kai said.

Quick, Who the fuck is Quick? I asked.

You know from out north, Donnie Lil brother, juju said.

What the fuck is he looking for me for? I asked.

They both shrugged their shoulders.

Ayee baby, I gotta make a run right quick, I said bending down to kiss Cha, and Lexis.

OK don't take too long, I love you, she said.

I love y'all too, I said before leaving.

What he say? I asked juju, and Kai once we got outside.

He came to the spot looking for you, he said to call this number, juju said handing me a piece of paper.

I called the number, he picked up on the third ring.

Who this? he asked picking up the phone.

I heard you was looking for me, I said.

He paused for a min, then laughed, yes indeed, we need to talk, where can we meet, he said.

Since you know where my spot at, I'll meet you there in 30, I said hanging up the phone.

I hoped in my car and followed them there. I called this young cat named Skippy from down the block, that was the lookout for me. I told him to be on the lookout for Quick, so he wants try no funny shit. I told T-bone the guy that worked the front door to only let Quick in, if he brings anybody they gotta wait outside.

What yall think this nigga want, I asked Kai, and juju as we waited in the office.

That nigga got the whole north side on lock, so he can't be tryna talk business, it gotta be beef, Kai said.

For what tho, we on two different sides of town, so I know I'm not stepping on his toes, I said.

A tap at the door drew our attention, juju got up to open it.

Wats good, quick said walking inside.

What up, I said back.

Yo, we finna run up the block, Kai said as he and juju got up and left.

What we need to discuss, I asked Quick, as I leaned forward on my desk.

You owe me an apology, I don't tolerate disrespect, and you disrespected me in the worst way, He said serious as hell.

What the fuck are you talking about, I asked.

My ol lady told me y'all had a run in, she said you called her out her name, and put your hands on her, he said.

You are talking about Leslie, I asked.

He nodded his head, and I laughed.

So, what we got beef over a female now, I asked.

Naw but you owe her an apology, he said.

Man look, yo gal disrespected me in my house, I ain't apologizing for shit, and if you don't like it, the both of y'all can stay the fuck away from my side of town, I got shit to tend to so you can hit the door with that bullshit you talking homeboy, I said frustrated.

He laughed as he stood up, that's cool but keep in mind I know where yo bitch stay, yo ol lady too, he said heading towards the door.

And if you even try to get close to her I'm going after yo mama ol bitch ass nigga, I said as he left.

My mind begin to race, I can't have Cha and my baby going home, and he know where she stay. I picked up the phone and called my mama.

Latoya's real estate agency, how may I help you, her receptionist picked up.

Yo Samantha is my mama there, I asked.

Yeah, boy hold on, she said putting me on hold.

Yes Langston, mama asked picking up the phone.

Was up mama, Chanel had the baby this morning, I said to her.

I know your sisters called me, I was on my way up there, what do you want, she asked me.

I need Chanel to move ASAP, I said.

What? She just moved there what happened, she asked.

I don't wanna talk about it ma, I need something today, I said getting aggravated.

Well, the only thing I have vacant is a four bedroom,

I'll take it, I said not even letting her finish.

Alright, I'll leave the paperwork with Samantha, and the keys, I'm going up to the hospital, she said.

Aight, tell her I'm on my way,

OK, and make sure you leave my money to, she said.

I got chu mama, I love you, I said to her.

I love you to son, she said before hanging up.

CHAPTER THRITY-TWO

Chanel:

Three days later we were in the car with Langston heading home.

Where are we going, I asked when I noticed we were going in the opposite direction from the house.

Home, he said while looking back and forth from his phone to the road.

I wanted to say something, but I really didn't feel like it. We pulled up to a nice house, it was bigger than ours but not that much bigger. He stopped the car cut it off and climbed out.

Come on baby, he said to me while taking Lexis car seat out.

I followed behind him, as he stuck a key in the door opening it.

Here, he said handing me the key.

Is this mine? I asked him.

Yeah, he said taking the baby out her seat, carrying her down the hall.

I followed him, I wanted to ask about this house and why we moved, but I was just happy to be home, and was ready to lay down. He walked into the master bedroom, kicked his shoes off, and climbed in the bed with Lexis up under him.

Come here girl, he said to me as I stood in the doorway.

I wanna take a shower first, I said looking around the room.

I've been in the hospital for three days, and he has managed to move everything in our old house here. I walked to the dresser drawer, and pulled out some panties, with one of his t-shirts. I showered then climbed in next to him, Lexis was no longer in the bed with him, she was now in her bassinet that sat beside the bed. He wrapped his arms around me and pulled me close.

You smell good girl, he said in a sleepy tone.

Thanks, I said as his hand slipped down to my ass.

I felt his stick getting on hard, I wanted to stop him, but I was scared he would leave and go lay up under Yotti. He picked up his ringing phone and looked at the caller Id before answering.

Wasup baby, he answered the phone.

Bring your ass home now, she said before hanging up in his face.

I wanted to scream at the sound of her voice. He climbed out the bed and put his shoes on. He walked over to Lexis, and gently picked her up. He looked at her with a smile on his face, before kissing her small cheek. He laid her down and walked towards me. He bent down to kiss my lips, but I turned my head. He sighed and left without saying a word to me.

Yotti:

I was online booking party reservation for boss's birthday, while talking on the phone to MyMy.

Who is Leslie? I asked her.

That's Marco's cousin, she called him saying she got into it with hustla, and that he called her a bitch, and hit her, MyMy said.

Let me call you back, I said as I heard the front door open.

Who the fuck is Leslie? I asked the minute I saw his face.

Huh, he asked looking confused.

I didn't stutter, you heard me, I said folding my arms across my chest.

Just sum broad, why you ask me that, he said staring at me.

What she do to you for you to put your hands on her, I asked him.

She was spreading rumors bae, it's not that serious, he said.

Obviously, it was, for you to put your hands on her, I said.

I didn't touch her, so she is spreading rumors again, he said.

I just looked at him, the shit he was saying is not adding up, but I will find out the truth sooner or later.

Where boss at, he asked heading towards our bedroom.

Sleep, I need some money for his party, I said following him to the room.

Aight, come here, he said taking his shoes off laying across the bed.

The minute I laid down; I smelled a fragrance I have never worn before.

What bitch you been up under, I asked sitting up.

What? Wat are you talking about now man, he asked sounding frustrated.

You smell like some shit I don't even where, I yelled, he was pissing me off.

I went to see mama today, why the fuck are you tripping? he yelled back.

I didn't know if he was lying or telling the truth, but I didn't feel like arguing with him. I went upstairs to get boss clothes out for daycare the next morning. I went back downstairs got my clothes out and showered. I climbed in bed, as he took a shower. When he got out, he climbed in bed, he wrapped his arms around me pulling me close.

Langston, I slightly whispered his name.

Yes, he said while rubbing my stomach.

Are you cheating on me? I asked him I just wanted to know the truth.

No Yatise I'm not cheating on you, you finna have my daughter, and you gone be my wife one day, ain't nothing out there worth fucking that up, he said.

I turned to face him; I kissed his lips as his hands gripped my ass.

I love you daddy, I said.

I love you too girl, he said.

One week later.

Boss's party was a success, this year for my birthday I wasn't really in the mood to celebrate.

Auntie was going to pick boss up from school, so I planned to go get some last-minute stuff for the baby. I pulled up at Langston's spot to get some money. I climbed out the car, and walked up the stairs, four men wearing ski mask jumped out pointing their guns in my face.

Knock on the door, one of them said grabbing my arm.

He sounded familiar, but my mind was racing so fast, I couldn't put a face to his voice. He pushed me closer towards the door, while stepping to the side, so whoever opened the door wouldn't see him. Tears rolled down my face, as I knocked on the door.

Hustla:

I was Counting the last of the money my boys just dropped off when I heard a knock at the door. Today was the first of the month, so everybody was out making money. Yotti called and told me she was on her way, so I knew it was her.

Was up girl, I said opening the screen door.

I noticed she had tears in her eyes, but before I could say anything I was hit in the face with the butt of a gun. I stumbled back, as blood gushed out my mouth. They pushed Yotti to the side, causing her to fall. The taller one to the right lifted his strap and shot me in the leg.

Aaahhhh shit, I hollered out.

Shut the fuck up nigga where the work at, one of the other guys yelled at me.

Fuck you, I said thru gritted teeth.

The one that shot me nodded towards the back, as the other two went to the back.

Take whatever you find, the leader said.

Nigga you might as well kill me, cause on my daughter if you don't, bitch you mine, I said looking at the one that shot me.

For some reason this nigga wouldn't talk. He lifted his gun and shot me in the arm.

Fuck, I hollered out, as he lifted his gun aiming it at my head.

Noooo, please don't kill my husband, Yotti yelled out as she jumped in front of me.

The one that held the gun lowered it away from Yotti.

Fuck them, the other one said aiming his gun at us, as the two men came from the back with duffle bags.

He still didn't open his mouth, he just shook his head, and nodded towards the door and they left.

The end!!!!

ABOUT THE AUTHOR

LaCoya Foxx better known as Coya was born and raised in Nashville Tn on May 9, 1991. She is a person of many talents such as singing rapping and of course writing. Her passion for writing came at the age of 13 when she read her first urban novel. She started off with short stories, that she would write on notebook paper. Then at the age 15 she wrote this book, "Daddy's Destruction". You're probably wondering why it took 15 years to release this book, well you can put the blame on her. She spent years of doubting her talent, every time she would reread the book she felt that it wasn't good enough until one day Her sister told her " you think it's not good enough because you're 30 reading what a 15 year old wrote, of course the book is going to seem immature to you, publish the book and once you publish your latest books your readers will see you growth as a writer" and she was right I say that to say no matter what your story is or how much you feel like you're not good enough at something go for it your craft can only get better we are our biggest haters and it's time to stop hating